Por SS
Porte, Barbara Ann.
He's sorry, she's sorry,
   they're sorry, too$ 13.00

W9-CLO-776

He's Sorry, She's Sorry, They're Sorry, Too

He's Sorry, She's Sorry, They're Sorry, Too

Stories by Barbara Ann Porte

Hanging Loose Press
Brooklyn, New York

Copyright © 1998 by Barbara Ann Porte

Published by Hanging Loose Press, 231 Wyckoff Street, Brooklyn, NY 11217. All rights reserved. No part of this book may be reproduced without the publisher's written permission, except for brief quotations in reviews. This book is fiction. The characters and events in it are imagined and any resemblance to real people, living or dead, is coincidental.

Printed in the United States of America
10 9 8 7 6 5 4 3 2 1

Some stories in this book first appeared in slightly different form and/or with different titles in the following magazines: "The Galloper," *Green's Magazine*, Winter, 1987; "Dr. Akiri," *Karamu* Fall 1985; "American Pastorale," *San Jose Studies*, Winter, 1987; "Growing Pains," *Earth's Daughters*, 1983; "He's Sorry, She's Sorry, They're Sorry, Too," *13th Moon*, 1994. "How a Basement Impostor was Finally Disposed of, and a Wife Remained Faithful" (1994), Varicella/Variations (1996), and "Claudia" (1995) were all originally published in *Hanging Loose* magazine.

Hanging Loose Press thanks the Literature Program of the New York State Council on the Arts for a grant in support of the publication of this book.

Cover art by Rosemary Feit Covey
Cover design by Caroline Drabik

Library of Congress Cataloging-in-Publication Data

Porte, Barbara Ann.
  He's sorry, she's sorry, they're sorry, too / Barbara Ann Porte.
    p.   cm.
  ISBN 1-882413-47-4. -- ISBN 1-882413-46-6 (pbk.)
  I. Title.
PS3566.06293H4   1998
813'.54--dc21   97-42681
                                                      CIP

Produced at The Print Center, Inc., 225 Varick St., New York, NY 10014, a non-profit facility for literary and arts-related publications. (212) 206-8465

CONTENTS

for Floyd

How a Basement Impostor Was Finally Disposed of, and a Wife Remained Faithful

(A modern Konjaku tale, the Japanese Konjaku Mono-gatari, a collection of 1,000 tales, being a work of the 11th century)

Ages ago, in this neighborhood, an animal of disputed dimensions, having made its way into a basement, caused a temporary rift between a husband and his wife. It happened like this.

Mr. and Mrs. Sugimoto had been living in their new house for several months when Mrs. Sugimoto first noticed that the hard, wrapped candies she kept in a glass dish on a living room table seemed to be disappearing at a rate disproportionate to what she and her husband were eating. Even more mysterious, she sometimes found one or two, in various stages of unwrap, lying on the hardwood floor beside the door leading to the basement steps. At about the same time, she also found herself sweeping up fine wood shavings in that same vicinity.

"I think some sort of animal is living in our basement," she told Mr. Sugimoto, preferring not to name it.

Mr. Sugimoto had for some time suspected the same, the cause in his case being peanuts missing from a jar he kept atop his desk in the modest home office he'd set up in the basement. Stranger yet, he sometimes found empty shells in his wastebasket he'd never put there. He hadn't mentioned it to his wife, certain he knew how she'd react. Nor was he wrong.

"You've got to do something," she told him.

"Yes," he said. "First thing tomorrow I'll buy a trap."

"No," Mrs. Sugimoto replied, confirming his fear. "You don't understand. I want you to go downstairs and do something *now*. I don't want a furry creature living in my basement. And anyway, it knows how to climb stairs." Even as she spoke Mrs. Sugimoto was rummaging in her laundry room off the kitchen. Taking what was there — a pair of her husband's sweat socks, and a large Turkish bath towel — she stuffed them into the considerable crack between the door and the floor. She didn't like to think of some strange animal, lying on its back, hard candy in its paws, squeezing underneath the door.

Well, Mr. Sugimoto didn't like thinking about that either. He knew rodents harbored fleas that transmitted terrible diseases. There was the one benefit, of course. It kept his wife out of his office, preventing her from dusting and straightening his papers. Even so, first thing the next morning, Mr. Sugimoto bought two mouse traps, baited them with cheese, and set them on the steps leading up from the basement.

Several days passed, and nothing had happened. Then, one morning as Mr. Sugimoto was heading downstairs to check his traps, Mrs. Sugimoto said, "Maybe you should try peanuts instead, or hard candy." Her husband glared at her.

"How did you get to be such an expert on trapping?" he wondered aloud, though under his breath. Still, that night he took her advice and used peanuts.

In the morning, when he inspected his traps, he found both had been sprung. The peanuts were gone, but he had not caught any animal. At exactly the same time Mr. Sugimoto was discovering this, Mrs. Sugimoto was making up her mind to remove the rolled up towel and socks she'd stuffed beneath the door.

"I'm really being foolish. There's probably nothing down there. This is a clear case of overreacting," she told herself, walking toward the stairway. She picked up the towel her husband had pushed aside, and began to unroll it. That was when she noticed both socks were gone, except for a few bright threads that trailed from the door. Half the towel, it turned out, also was missing, leaving the remaining half with a long, jagged, saw-toothed edge, clearly a sign of some awful, nocturnal struggle. Mrs. Sugimoto was horrified. Even Mr. Sugimoto looked surprised when she showed him.

"I think you'd better buy a larger trap," she said. Mr. Sugimoto didn't say anything. He could see his wife was already upset enough for one morning. He kissed her goodbye, and left for work.

The rest of that day, Mrs. Sugimoto tried hard to imagine what sort of animal could possibly be lurking in her basement, and how had it gotten in? Well, of course it could have started out small, she reasoned, and just grown larger living downstairs. She considered a ferret. Perhaps an opossum?

"But how does it survive without water? There's nothing to drink down there," she inquired of Mr. Sugimoto when he arrived home that evening with a pair of rat traps.

"Oh yes, there is," Mr. Sugimoto replied. "Are you forgetting our sump pump? To a rodent it's as good as a spring-fed well." Right away, Mrs. Sugimoto pictured an otter, maybe a beaver, swimming up through their underground pipe, emerging in the basement.

Time passed. Mr. Sugimoto experimented with larger traps, and different bait. "I'm feeding rats in my basement," he'd mutter to himself, when he found his traps emptied and sprung.

"Maybe we should get a cat, or borrow one," Mrs. Sugimoto suggested, but Mr. Sugimoto believed that animals did not belong in houses, living with people. "There's one living in the house with us now. It's only a question of what kind," Mrs. Sugimoto pointed out. For her part, she'd removed all food from view, and also fortified her Turkish towel barricade.

"You know, we'll never sell the house this way," she warned Mr. Sugimoto. "People coming to look will want to know why we keep towels on the floor. Prospective buyers do not like to hear there is some furry animal living in the basement." Well, she was speaking hypothetically. They had no plans to move out. They'd barely moved in, but Mrs. Sugimoto was familiar with the principles of property values. She discussed the problem with relatives and neighbors; even strangers were not immune from her query. "What do you think can be living in my basement?" she'd ask plaintively. This became an ever-increasing sore point between Mr. and Mrs. Sugimoto.

"It's nobody's business," he told her. "It's always a mistake to tell everything you know."

Next door to the Sugimotos, there lived an elderly gentleman, Monsieur Jourdan, a widower from France, with whom Mrs. Sugimoto had become friendly. He had been raised in Provence, and liked to pass the time of day relating tales he had heard as a child. Mrs. Sugimoto, perhaps by way of holding up her end of the conversation, kept him up to date on what was going on in her basement.

"You know, I think your problem isn't an animal," Monsieur Jourdan said one day. "I think you may have a ghost in your basement."

"A ghost?" said Mrs. Sugimoto. It was not something she had even considered.

"Oh, yes," said Monsieur Jourdan. "I once heard of something similar. A relative of mine played a part in it, and it's a true story." Then he told it to her.

"It seems at one time a certain Monsieur Vidal died, leaving no family behind. His house remained empty for over a year. The same as yours," said Monsieur Jourdan. "When a couple was finally found to move in, they didn't stay very long. It was too noisy there. Every night, just as they were falling asleep, they'd be awakened by strange sounds, as of someone, or something, shuffling around. As hard as they tried, they never could discover where the noises came from. A short time later, they moved away. 'That house is haunted,' said the neighbors. Afterward, no one wanted to live there."

"So, how did it turn out?" asked Mrs. Sugimoto.

"That's where my relative came in," said M. Jourdan. "He did not believe in ghosts. He made up his mind to stay overnight in that house and see what was what. He took with him his old army saber, and a lantern whose light he concealed beneath his cloak. He stretched himself out beneath the stairway. No sooner had he started falling asleep, however, than he was awakened by noises, as of someone, or something, shuffling around. Before you could blink, he was on his feet, his lantern uncovered. But what do you think he saw? Only this: three very large rats, running up the stairs. No ghost at all."

Mrs. Sugimoto laughed. "Yes, but why do you think my problem is a ghost, then?"

"Ah, don't you see. Stories are like dreams. They go by contraries. My countrymen thought ghosts, but it turned out rats. For sure, your animal will turn out otherwise."

That night, thinking it was a funny story, Mrs. Sugimoto told it to her husband. As time went by, however, she reflected on it. Mrs. Sugimoto's own maternal grandmother had grown up in the snow country of Japan. She told stories, too. Some of them were about ghosts. Some of the ghosts also were tricksters: foxes, badgers, or some other animal. The existence of such beings, then, was by no means a foreign subject to Mrs. Sugimoto. Also, there was this. Though the thought of a rodent in her basement dismayed Mrs. Sugimoto, she was not in other ways a timid person. Now, she told herself, a ghost would truly be something to see. Therefore, a week or so later, when Mr. Sugimoto left home on a long business trip, Mrs. Sugimoto made up her mind to stay overnight in the basement and see what was what. She took with her a sharp sushi knife, and also her husband's multipurpose three-way lantern, with its krypton spotlight bulb, a blinking amber beam to call for help, and soft area illumination. There was an AM/FM radio on the opposite end. She went downstairs, and stretched out on her husband's chair to watch.

After some time had gone by, Mrs. Sugimoto began feeling drowsy. Her head nodded, and her eyes closed. No sooner did she start to fall asleep, however, than she was awakened by noises, as of someone, or something, moving about in the basement. At the same time, she thought she also heard music, and only for a second wondered if, perhaps, it was coming from the radio end of her lantern. Then, almost before you could blink, Mrs. Sugimoto was on her feet, her krypton spotlight bulb switched on, and her sushi knife in her hand.

"I'm armed," she announced in her loudest voice, trying to sound brave, and also look taller. She waved the knife about in the air, and directed the krypton beam along the plaster walls, and into the corners. She was herself blinded, at first, by so much sudden light, but when she finally could see, this was what she saw. A man was leaning gracefully against the farthest wall, beneath a window well. He was pale and slim, with a narrow face and pearly white teeth, and very good-looking. He lowered the bamboo flute he'd been playing, and bowed deeply. That was when Mrs. Sugimoto noticed he had on her husband's socks, and also the missing portion of her towel was draped across his back. She could also see, then, he had long, lustrous hair, dark chestnut-red, held back by frayed thread in a ponytail. For goodness' sake, she thought. There is a homeless man living in my basement. A musician, no less. Right away, she struck up a conversation.

"How nicely you play," she said to the man. "I think music is what I've been missing. See, my husband is tuneless, entirely. He cannot so much as keep time, even by clapping. Just my singing gives him a headache. You can forget about dancing." Well, she'd been alone all day in the house with no one to talk to. She was ready for a bit of chitchat, no matter with whom.

"Ah," said the man, nodding in an understanding fashion. One thing led to another. Mrs. Sugimoto was a hospitable person, not about to put a homeless person out after dark, and her husband wasn't at home to consult. Therefore, she did the only thing that came to mind.

"Would you like something to eat?" she asked the musician. Of course he would. It soon became a habit, and Mrs. Sugimoto increasingly looked forward to late nights spent downstairs. Each evening she prepared two dinners, fish fried in peanut oil and rice cakes, for instance, candies for dessert, then carried them to the basement. They dined together by lantern light, set on soft area illumination, and listened to the radio. Afterward, he played his flute, and Mrs. Sugimoto brushed up on her dancing. When she felt ready, she turned the radio back on, and he lay down his instrument. They danced together. Both were very fine dancers. They danced the rumba and waltz, the tango and fox trot. Once, unable to resist, Mrs. Sugimoto reached out a hand and grasped her partner's long sleek hair. He stopped at once, and stepped back.

"Don't do that!" he said, and she didn't, ever again.

Weeks went by in this way, until one day it was time for Mrs. Sugimoto's husband to return from his business trip. "If I were you, I'd lay low for a bit," Mrs. Sugimoto warned the man in her basement. "I probably won't get back for a while." Strange to say, it slipped her mind entirely to provide him any food to tide him over while she was gone, and he was too polite to remind her.

The following afternoon, Mr. Sugimoto came home. "Wow," he said, coming through the doorway, kissing his wife. "I really missed you." Mrs. Sugimoto smiled, inscrutably.

"What's in that package?" she asked, pointing.

"Ah," said Mr. Sugimoto, and unwrapped a wire cage. "See, it's big enough for catching any animal that may have moved into our basement. Well, unless it's a bear. The man who sold it to me once had a similar problem." Then he showed her how the spring-lock door at one end snapped shut when a lever was tripped, and how to release it. A second door at the opposite end fastened with a latch.

"Um," said Mrs. Sugimoto, regarding the cage warily. After dinner, she watched as Mr. Sugimoto baited the trap with peanuts and left open the spring-lock door. Just before he carried the trap downstairs to set it in the basement, Mrs. Sugimoto remembered, and slipped a bit of leftover fish and a piece of rice cake inside. She'd already made up her mind to keep away from the basement. She was happily married, after all, plus a person her age could engage in only so much dancing. The Sugimotos turned in early that night. Well, after such a long business trip, you can imagine.

In the middle of the night, Mr. Sugimoto sat up in bed, and turned on his light. "Do you hear something?" he asked his wife.

"Like what?" she said.

"Nothing," he said. "I must have been dreaming." He didn't want to alarm her with talk of music coming from the basement, and she was not about to mention it, either. They both went back to sleep.

First thing the next morning, Mr. Sugimoto went downstairs to check on his trap. He called excitedly upstairs to his wife to come join him.

"For goodness' sake," she said, examining the empty cage carefully. All the peanuts were gone, and so were the fish and rice cake. Both doors were wide open. Alongside the cage lay the remnants of Mr. Sugimoto's socks, neatly folded; and many long strands of dark hair, that looked suspiciously familiar to Mrs. Sugimoto, trailed on the floor, as though left behind by some animal in a hurry.

"Well, that's that," said Mr. Sugimoto. "It was probably a badger, or even a fox. One thing's for sure, it's not coming back. It would be too embarrassed to return without its tail, believe me." Mrs. Sugimoto believed him.

16

"Well, the fox trot, no wonder," she murmured to herself.

"Say what?" asked her husband.

"Oh nothing. I was just thinking out loud," she told him. The question that puzzled her, though, was why such a musical trickster had chosen her basement to visit. He could have chosen anyone's. No doubt he had his reasons.

Some days later, Mrs. Sugimoto related everything to M. Jourdan. "I'm not surprised," he said. "See, it goes to show a person shouldn't spend too much time in a basement. As for staying overnight in one, don't even consider it." Well, of course, Mrs. Sugimoto didn't.

Mr. Mabrey's Treatment

M r. Mabrey had been going for treatments. He thought of it as taking a cure. At fifty-six years old, he was in the process of reversing the sexual side effects of high blood pressure medicine. This was how it had come about: The Mabreys' former family doctor had died. His practice had been sold to a husband and wife from India. Almost immediately, they had relocated it to a lower-rent, more ethnic neighborhood. The Mabreys went along. Why not? After all, we aren't prejudiced people, Mrs. Mabrey reasoned. Still, Mr. Mabrey resisted going.

He put off and put off his annual visit. Even after Mrs. Mabrey had gone so far as to set up an appointment for him, something had come up at work, and he'd had to cancel it. The real reason, though, Mr. Mabrey couldn't find time to go, was this: He was reluctant to take the chance of being examined by a female physician. He was even more reluctant to admit this to his wife. He knew she'd laugh at him. In fact, suspecting this to be his reason, she'd laughed at him already. Only when he was down to his last few beta blocker tablets, and could no longer get his prescription refilled by telephone, did he agree to his wife's setting up a new appointment. He didn't specify with which doctor, and neither did she. As it turned out, he saw the husband, who worked only two evenings a week in that office and had a second practice of his own elsewhere in the city.

"Ramadan, here; it means the hot month," the doctor said by way of introduction, holding out his hand, referring to his name. Its significance escaped Mr. Mabrey at the time, though later he'd consider it. Proceeding from the handshake, this was how the visit went:

Top to bottom, inside out, Mr. Mabrey had never been so thoroughly examined. He had an EKG and chest x-ray (even though he'd never smoked), breathed into a hose to check his lung capacity, gave a urine sample and several vials of blood for testing, including HIV.

"Please not to worry, it's purely precautionary, only routine. Also, it's covered by insurance," Dr. Ramadan assured him. Certainly this last turned out to be true. So long as the Mabreys used the Ramadans, no matter how high the charges incurred, insurance paid them.

"Nothing owed," the doctors' receptionist told them every time.

"It's better than an HMO," the Mabreys said, explaining it to friends and relatives.

As Mr. Mabrey was buttoning his shirt following his examination, he mentioned to the doctor, "I think blood pressure is not my real problem. I think a young wife is my problem. A man should marry someone closer to his own age. Young women are always wanting to be 'doing it.' I am getting too old for all of that." Though Mrs. Mabrey was, indeed, younger than her husband by a decade, Mr. Mabrey meant what he said as a joke, or at least thought he did. Therefore, he was surprised when Dr. Ramadan took such inordinate interest in the matter.

"Yes," he said. "Loss of libido is often a side effect of the medicine. Then just cutting back is sometimes sufficient. We will try that first. You will take every day half your normal dose, then every other day, then finally nothing at all. We will see how you do. But you should not worry anyway. Your problem is easy to treat. I can give you shots, one, two, three; nothing to it. Excellent results every time. You will feel like a teenager again, believe me."

When Mr. Mabrey got home that night, he told his wife. "One shot a month, testosterone, and I can be like a young man again. I tried to tell the doctor I was joking."

"Yes?" said Mrs. Mabrey, and waited with interest to hear more.

But all Mr. Mabrey said was, "Time for bed." Then he got ready, climbed in, and fell asleep immediately. He stayed that way until morning.

Over breakfast Mrs. Mabrey asked, "How much would the shots cost?"

"What shots?" asked Mr. Mabrey.

"The testosterone shots," she said, surprised how quickly he'd forgotten.

"I didn't ask. Maybe you should call and discuss it with the doctor," Mr. Mabrey told her. Though they both spoke jestingly, the question lingered.

When Mr. Mabrey went back to his doctor the following month to check on his blood pressure, which was doing fine, the doctor recalled their previous conversation. "Ready for shots?" he asked. "They're working one hundred percent, believe me. Nothing to lose. Treatment entirely covered by insurance. Think about it. We can start next time if you like."

"You have nothing to lose," Mrs. Mabrey said when her husband told her. "You can always stop if you find the treatment isn't for you." She sounded a lot like the doctor. Even so, she didn't persist. Now that Mr. Mabrey had begun cutting back on his beta blocker medicine, her own sex life had improved sufficiently. "After all, I'm not a spring chicken myself anymore," she told her sister on the telephone. Therefore, when Mr. Mabrey, on his third visit to the doctor, said, "I've decided to try your treatment," he was speaking entirely on his own.

"Yes, very good. You won't be sorry; I promise you that," Dr. Ramadan said happily, preparing the injection right away. Afterward, he patted Mr. Mabrey on his shoulder. "Come back in one month," he told him, his tone a bit tittery.

Mr. Mabrey didn't discuss this visit with his wife. He thought he'd wait and see how the treatments went, and then surprise her.

To say that they went well would be an understatement. Mrs. Mabrey was first surprised, then worried. She thought perhaps Mr. Mabrey wasn't up to such strenuous exercise. "It's no wonder you find it hard to get out of bed in the morning. I think people our age aren't in shape for so many new positions. We've never been *that* athletic," she told him. Her warnings didn't last. Not long after, Mrs. Mabrey landed in the hospital with female complaints: cysts on her ovaries, uterine fibroids, abnormal bleeding.

"It's nothing at all to do with sex; very common problems in women your age," Mrs. Dr. Ramadan assured her. "You'll be better than new after surgery, nothing to worry about. We'll give you an estrogen patch right away. No more uterus, no need for progesterone. Your bones will stay strong, your membranes moist, facial hair will never be a problem. You'll feel like a young woman again, believe me."

Why wouldn't Mrs. Mabrey believe her? Mrs. Mabrey was a modern person who kept up with science. Even so, her thoughts turned back to her mother's nurse and a conversation they'd had long ago. Mrs. Mabrey's mother was 83 at the time, with ovarian cancer. The nurse, middle-aged and dark-complexioned, was from Nicaragua. She told Mrs. Mabrey, "My sister died of that. She was forty-six. She always blamed her husband."

"Her husband?" said Mrs. Mabrey.

"Oh yes. She always said he worked her too hard." Then the nurse had ducked her head in embarrassment, giggled and gone into another room. Mrs. Mabrey had smiled to herself at such superstition. Of course she knew better.

In her head she still knew better. "Absolutely no connection with sex," Mrs. Dr. Ramadan had told her. Nevertheless, lying there in her hospital bed, worried and in pain, exactly as that nurse's sister, in her heart she blamed her husband. Shots, sex, all those topsy-turvy positions, ridiculous for people our age; just see where it's gotten me.

Mrs. Mabrey was not the only one who blamed her husband. Mr. Mabrey blamed himself. "You mustn't feel guilty," Mrs. Mabrey's Dr. Ramadan told him, meeting him for the first time in the hallway outside Mrs. Mabrey's hospital room. "Trust me, sex is irrelevant." She was speaking of course only of sex between the two Mabreys. "Feeling guilty is the worst thing you can do," she assured him. "It will not help your wife at all." Mr. Mabrey guessed from this that she knew all about his treatment.

"Ah," he said and blushed. Immediately he trusted her. She looked so scientific in her doctor clothes. Also very sexy. Mr. Mabrey could not get over how desirable a woman could look in a white doctor coat, navy skirt, high-heeled shoes, and a stethoscope. Of course it was also true, in any attire, Dr. Ramadan would be good looking. She was fine-boned and slender, with well-shaped legs; huge, recessed eyes; and sensuous rubicund lips. She had smooth, gold-tinted skin, and a thick black braid that hung, so seductively, down her back, stopping at just that place where her buttocks began curving out, obvious even beneath the doctor coat.

In the sort of moment that passes like a flash, Mr. Mabrey wondered what she could possibly see in her husband: a tiny, often jittery man, who spoke in a high-pitched voice, and sometimes giggled giving shots. But then he thought, well, India, after all. Weren't arranged marriages still popular there? And weren't Indians known for being practical people? What could be more practical than a marriage arranged between doctors?

"Perhaps we could discuss my wife's condition over coffee?" Mr. Mabrey suggested.

"Yes, why not?" Dr. Ramadan replied. She'd been on call the night before, and was only now finishing her rounds. She could use a bit of a break. Besides which, she took an interest in her husband's work. His patients were usually so peppy.

"I'm a peppy person myself," she sometimes told them. "Tea would be fine," she said to Mr. Mabrey.

A few minutes later, seated across from him in the hospital cafeteria, Dr. Ramadan sipped tea and sighed audibly. "You are fortunate having my husband for your physician," she said. "He is a very fine doctor, totally dedicated. Day and night he works hard in both offices. He makes his patients like young men again. But he himself doesn't take treatment. He wants no distraction from work. When he comes home, always late, he barely has energy to eat. Then right away afterward he falls into bed and immediately is asleep. I, too, work hard. But see, a woman like me always needs some diversion."

Why did hearing this so excite Mr. Mabrey? Was it only the effect of all those shots? Or was he, too, perhaps in need of diversion. A sick wife to worry about, hospital bills, and now such good news—he wasn't to blame for his wife's condition. More than all of this, though, was the thrill that swept through him imagining a dalliance with a doctor. Who'd know more about the human body and its sexual responses to tactile stimuli? Mr. Mabrey felt tingly just thinking about it. He pressed his knees together in an effort to contain himself, and blushed again. Dr. Ramadan squeezed his thigh with one hand, and laughed.

"Nothing to be embarrassed about," she told him. "I could tell just by looking, you'd be a good patient. Isn't it so?"

It certainly seemed to be. Nor was Mr. Mabrey disappointed in his expectations. Even taking into account the cumulative effect of his monthly shots, Mr. Mabrey was amazed. Scientists certainly are imaginative people, he thought. His joy was exquisite. Still, there was his age. Even the best treatment can only go so far. Times came he faltered.

"You've worn me out," he'd say, disappointed, unable to keep up. But Dr. Ramadan would not hear of it.

"Don't be silly," she'd say, rinsing him off with a hot cloth she kept prepared for that purpose. "There's always more than one way." Then she'd turn him, or herself, around and lean down, and in just that second that she did, Mr. Mabrey would think of Eastern philosophy. Many ways to one God. Nirvana. From where did such thoughts come? Mr. Mabrey was not a religious person. Yet as Dr. Ramadan worked over him with her doctor mouth and doctor tongue, her doctor throat and doctor fingers, he certainly attained that blissful state, whatever its name. At such times Dr. Ramadan would sit back, toss her tousled braid over one shoulder, look at him and laugh.

"What do you think? Who's the better doctor, I or my husband?" she'd ask. Naturally at these times Mr. Mabrey always was partial. One time she told him, "I think you're the one with the power; for sure a magician. When I am doing this to you, I become like a musician, a basuri player with superior hand and mouth coordination. But see, in real life, just keeping time can be a problem."

"Really?" said Mr. Mabrey. He had no idea what a basuri was, but it sounded exotic. Why had his wife never told him anything similar? Eventually he looked it up: a reed pipe, sometimes two joined at the mouthpiece, to be fingered and blown. By then Mr. Mabrey was less certain that he liked this image of himself. Also by then his wife was home from the hospital, recovering fast from her surgery, and claiming attention. Plus there was this: Mr. Mabrey had discovered some new information about Dr. Ramadan. She was, in real life, a musician.

"Oh yes, very superior playing, concert caliber," her husband told Mr. Mabrey during his final visit. "First instrument is the basuri, but she is playing also sitar, flute, oboe, pungi, sarangi, whatever you like. All very fine instruments." He was explaining why his wife didn't work nights. "Every evening she must be practicing; public performances coming up. Well, enough chit-chat about music. But you see why I am having to cut back on patients. Good help is too hard to find. No more time for those already cured like you," he said, and poked Mr. Mabrey in his middle. "But please not to worry.

Any recurrence of problem, I am referring you to my brother-in-law, excellent, very good doctor, all work guaranteed, in the city. So for now, finished, over, through, good-bye, good luck, give my regards to Mrs. Mabrey, please." Mr. Mabrey wondered just then exactly how much did this doctor know, and since when.

"Nothing owed," the receptionist told him as Mr. Mabrey passed by her going out the door. She glanced at his records. "I guess we won't be seeing you any more," she added, filing his folder in the 'inactive patients' drawer. Mr. Mabrey, lost in reflection, didn't notice she was sneering.

"Imagine, a basuri player," he was saying to himself. "There's no trusting such a person who claims to be unmusical. A woman who will lie about one thing will lie about another." This Mr. Mabrey believed. Right away he resumed feeling guilty, only now he had reason. It had the effect on him of making him behave with special tenderness toward his wife.

"My goodness, what's got into you! I hope you're not still taking shots," she said to him that night.

"Oh no. That's over, finished, through. I think such treatment isn't for people our age." Mrs. Mabrey could not agree more. Beside her own health, now that Mr. Mabrey no longer took blood pressure medicine, she worried about the effect on his heart of too much sex.

While the Mabreys were having their conversation, across town a different conversation was going on. The Drs. Ramadan's receptionist was on the telephone complaining to her roommate. "It's so unfair. Why does she get all the peppy patients while I have to make do with leftovers? Then when their treatments are finished they're gone, poof, just like that. We never see them again. Not that I'd want to. I like peppy men too. It's so humiliating. I'm sure I'm as peppy as she. I'm certainly younger. What can she possibly do in bed that I don't?"

"I'm sure it's nothing to do with you," her roommate told her. "It's only that she's a doctor. You'd be surprised how ga-ga some men can get over a woman carrying a stethoscope, dressed in a white doctor coat." What surprised the receptionist was hearing that her roommate knew this.

"Ummm," she said. She felt certain there was more. After all, didn't she sometimes, also, dress up in a white doctor coat and carry a stethoscope? Just not in the office. Of course she didn't play the basuri. She couldn't even so much as pat her feet in time to music. It did sometimes cross her mind to wonder if rhythmical proficiency carried over into bed.

By the time she hung up the telephone, she'd decided; enough was enough. She wasn't one to take such treatment lying down. She drafted two letters. The first she mailed to patients the next day from the office. The second was her resignation. Naturally, she would have preferred staying on to see how things turned out, but though she was only a receptionist, she wasn't stupid.

Some time went by. Life resumed its normal course, more or less, for the Mabreys. Mr. Mabrey had found a new doctor, a middle-aged man who he hoped would outlive him. The idea of ever having to break in another new physician was more than he could bear. Mrs. Mabrey understood how he felt.

"Yes, it's why I'm sticking with my old Dr. Ramadan," she told him. "She knows my whole body, inside and out." Well, of course she knew Mr. Mabrey's body inside and out, too, but now that Mrs. Mabrey was recovered, Mr. Mabrey had no good reason for visits with her doctor. He worried how she'd take the news.

"Yes, of course, over, finished, fine." She wasn't in the least surprised. She knew what it meant when patients stopped treatments. This wasn't her first, it wouldn't be her last time. She was glad she had her concert series coming up. It would fill her evenings nicely in the meanwhile. She'd arranged to play percussion. "It will be a good change of pace for me," she told her husband.

As for Mrs. Mabrey, she couldn't remember ever feeling

better. "I feel wonderful," she told her sister. "Also, I don't think that much about sex anymore. It's so liberating."

"Well of course it is," said her sister. "Without all those extra parts to worry about, you're more self-sufficient."

"Ah," said Mrs. Mabrey, who had thought it was the estrogen. She may have been right, or maybe her sister was, or possibly it was some combination. On the other hand, there also was this: Mrs. Mabrey had a new outside interest. She was learning how to play the oboe.

"There's nothing like music to take a person's mind off her surgery and prevent side effects. I'm recommending it to all my patients," Dr. Ramadan had told her. She also knew a teacher.

"Oh yes, my sister-in-law is a first-class musician, very superior, concert caliber. She's giving very excellent lessons." So now Mrs. Mabrey went once a week for instruction, and practiced every night in between, faithfully blowing and fingering.

"The oboe is a good instrument for a person like me," she told her husband. "It requires superior hand and mouth coordination. My teacher says I have that."

"Yes?" said her husband, and looked a bit wary. Well, he was also that minute opening the mail. He held out a letter for Mrs. Mabrey to see.

It was computer-printed on a half sheet of yellow paper, all in small caps. Mrs. Mabrey put on her glasses to read it. ***SPECIAL NOTICE***PLEASE TAKE HEED OF THE FOLLOWING appeared beneath the Ramadans' letterhead. Then came this message: DEAR PATIENT, IT HAS BEEN BROUGHT TO OUR ATTENTION THAT OUR FORMER RECEPTIONIST HAS BEEN SPREADING MALICIOUS RUMORS CONCERNING OUR PRACTICE. SHOULD ANY OF THESE RUMORS REACH YOU WE WOULD APPRECIATE YOUR LETTING US KNOW. IF YOU HAVE ANY QUESTIONS AT ALL PLEASE CONTACT OUR OFFICE. THANK YOU. Both doctors' names were printed at the bottom.

"I wonder what it means," said Mrs. Mabrey.

"Who knows?" said Mr. Mabrey, shrugging, though actually he did, having opened the mail on the day the receptionist's letter had arrived. He'd read the letter right away, then shredded and discarded it. Mrs. Mabrey was upstairs in bed that day still recovering from surgery. He'd seen no reason to disturb her.

"Maybe it has to do with how they handle patient insurance claims," Mrs. Mabrey mused now. "So much equipment, all that testing, never any bills." She wasn't complaining. In fact, she'd been relieved to see it was a notice, not a statement, they'd received. So far, her surgery hadn't cost them a penny. On the other hand, she did sometimes worry insurance would one day catch up with the Ramadans, and cause them to spend time in jail. Then Mrs. Mabrey would have to find herself a new doctor. Right now, she had no time to think about it. She was heading for the door, already late, on her way to take a music lesson.

"You know, I don't know what it is, but some days I feel I was born to play the oboe," she told her teacher that day. "It's such a romantic instrument."

"Yes?" said her teacher. She wasn't surprised. A lot of her patients felt that same way. Of course she meant students.

Meanwhile, Mr. Mabrey, home alone, re-read the notice, then tossed it out. "Ramadan, it means the hot month," flitted through his head. Already he'd forgotten where he'd heard it. He fixed himself tea and sipped it. Soon he was humming, an old carousel tune he hadn't thought of in years—something to do with love, a nickelodeon, and music, music, music. Ah, truly, he thought, a bit of song makes everything better. Mr. Mabrey turned on the radio, and patted his foot in time to the beat. He waited patiently for Mrs. Mabrey to get home. How happy he would be to see her.

Bad Hair Day

In South China, generally speaking, most people have enviable hair that doesn't require too much in the way of care to stay healthy. But just as everywhere, there are always some people who worry.

"Eat plenty of vegetables, drink lots of water. You don't want to end up like He," mothers often warn unmarried daughters. They mean He Xiangu, one of China's eight immortals, said to have been born in 700 A.D. in Guangdong with only six hairs sprouting from her head. Nor, despite all her best efforts, did she ever grow more. Yet in portraits she is always represented as having a full head of hair. How could this be?

Some say it was because the portraitists hoped to win favor through flattery. Others attribute it to the power of celestial illusion. But isn't it also possible that the truth regarding He is similar to the embarrassing case of Dr. Zhuo?

Dr. Zhuo was both a physician and an inventor. He came from the mountainous region of Zhejiang where people paid attention to plants and herbs, from which Dr. Zhuo produced numerous kinds of elixirs, syrups and potions. He specialized in finding cures for skin diseases. As such formulas take time to perfect, however, his wife raised chickens and pigs to support them in the meantime.

It happened that in a certain year in their village a baby was born with no hair. Nor did any grow in afterward. When it came time for him to start school, he hid himself instead of going, complaining that the other children made fun of him. *Baldy*, they called him, and so did most of the older villagers. It got so bad that the little boy would never go anywhere in the daytime. His parents didn't insist. They, too, were embarrassed by his condition. That was why it was past the third watch, nearly midnight, the first time they took the little boy to Dr. Zhuo's to see about a rash. All over the child's head, and even on his chin, were flat patches of dry skin that itched.

"Try this. It's new," Dr. Zhuo told them. It was something he had just invented. Not yet sure what it was good for, he was anxious to find out. If it doesn't help, it won't hurt either, he told himself, weighing out what seemed a good amount for one month's treatment. Its ingredients were natural, derived from local flora, and previously used effectively in other combinations: ginseng, milk vetch root, Chinese Angelica, dried ginger, Salvia root, walnut meat, safflower, and many more too numerous to mention, all dissolved in alcohol.

The parents were grateful. They took their little boy home to try out the medicine. Before the month was up, however, they returned, again in the dark, and not very happy. They wanted their money back. The medicine had done nothing to cure the rash, they said. But upon examining the child, Dr. Zhuo became excited. Here and there on his patient's head were prickly patches of sprouting hair, and on his chin was a miniature beard.

"He looks much better to me now," Dr. Zhuo told the little boy's parents. But he gave them a different medicine to try. "Proven highly effective for rashes. No extra charge," he said. As soon as they left, though, Dr. Zhuo began experimenting, making changes, adding this ingredient, reducing that one, testing everything on his wife's livestock. Finally, satisfied with the results, he named his new product "hair regeneration liniment" and began to advertise. "Works on the worst cases. Guaranteed 100 percent effective," he promised, pointing to his own thick head of hair as an example. He would have preferred using young Baldy, but the little boy's parents had taken him and moved to another village to avoid further embarrassment.

As it happened, the liniment did seem to work. Baldness all but disappeared in that village. Even old women's thinning hair grew in fuller when they borrowed their husbands' liniment. Word spread. Baldheaded people came from everywhere. Dr. Zhuo grew rich and famous. Now his wife didn't have to keep chickens and pigs anymore. How happy both of them were. Things might have gone on this way forever—if not for the earthquake.

Actually, as earthquakes go, this one wasn't too bad. Also, since its epicenter was some distance from the village where Dr. Zhuo lived, little damage was caused there. But even mild tremors can be frightening. First came a noise like thunder, then tables rocked, dishes broke, tree branches could be heard snapping. Dogs barked and roosters crowed even though it was still night. Not knowing what was happening, people ran outside in their sleepwear to consult with their neighbors. Only after the threat of danger seemed past and everyone was starting to go inside again, did anyone notice.

"Look at old Baldy," murmured some villagers, starting to point. "Who can it be? Hardly a strand of hair on his head." Others stared hard, astonished, then exclaimed in unison, "For goodness' sake, it's Dr. Zhuo." They were right. Dr. Zhuo had been losing his hair for some years. In the panic, though, he'd forgotten to put on his wig before going outside. Seeing him like this the villagers could hardly stop laughing.

"See Dr. Baldy! That barber ghost must have paid him a visit tonight," they told one another between fits of giggles. They meant of course the ghost known to shave people's heads while they sleep, leaving shiny bald places where hair will never grow back. The villagers thought this was very funny. But Dr. Zhuo didn't laugh. He felt so ashamed he packed his belongings and left town before morning. His wife went with him.

They took up residence in the city. Giving up his old way of life, Dr. Zhuo became a street barber. He carried his shop with him on a pole; a seat at one end, and a rack at the other holding everything he needed: a bowl, a water container, and a charcoal stove.

He was a walking advertisement for his work. "See how smooth and shiny," he'd say, patting his own head. "Even Luozi Daxian could not do better." He meant of course the former disciple of Laozi who gave up the religious life to become the patron of barbers, and whose birthday is celebrated by them every year.

As time passed, even if Barber Zhuo never made another fortune, he still did very well. He continued selling *hair regeneration liniment* on the side. "Guaranteed 90 percent effective," he promised. "Don't think there's no hope for baldness just because mine is an incurable case." He also held on to his wig. That way he could wear it should he ever have his portrait painted.

Varicella/Variations

chicken pox (varicella): once a common childhood disease for which there now exists a vaccine. Chicken pox is caused by the varicella-zoster virus, and is highly contagious. Its symptoms characteristically include mild fever, and eruptions of blisters and pimples which appear and then clear up in about a week, leaving scabs, but usually no scars. To the patient, the itching can seem intolerable, and is sometimes eased by bicarbonate of soda, oatmeal, or epsom salt baths. Complications, which are rare, include pneumonia, septicemia, encephalitis, and thrombocytopenia, any one of which can be fatal, and in the last case includes the possibility of the patient's bleeding to death internally from an insufficiency of platelets.

excerpted from *The Physician's Manual
of Infectious Diseases*

In order better to understand certain events, scientific and otherwise, it sometimes helps to put them in the framework of a coherent narrative. "So, what's the story?" we ask, ever hopeful there will be one, and that it will make sense. What if it doesn't?

* * *

Story number one. A pretty little girl with red curls once came down with chicken pox. You wouldn't think how the child looked would have much relevance, but as such information is included in nearly every story, it seemed worth putting down. In any event, her catching chicken pox wasn't surprising. She attended preschool, and chicken pox was going around. For a week or so she itched, was given oatmeal baths, and warned against scratching. Afterward, fully recovered, she returned to school. How happy her classmates and teachers were to see her. While she was out, they'd taken up reading fairy tales. Her very first day back, the class was listening to "Rapunzel." This is the tale in which two parents willingly agree to trade their not yet born daughter, eponymous protagonist of the story, to a witch, in exchange for the right to pick as many lettuce leaves from the witch's garden as they like. Pity the child with parents like that. The witch, on the other hand, after Rapunzel is born, tries hard and single-handedly to assure her well-being. Placing Rapunzel in a high tower, the witch holds onto the only key. How much safer could a child be? Even so, and despite the witch's best precautions, Rapunzel is eventually seduced by a prince and winds up pregnant, alone in the woods. Which goes to show that, in spite of our best efforts, children remain always at risk in the world.

prognosis: n.,a forecast; in *medicine,* a prediction of the probable course of a disease and the chances of recovery
> from *Webster's New World Dictionary*
> *of the American Language, College Edition*

To be a lover of stories requires some measure of patience, and also a stubborn belief that what starts out the same may next time turn out otherwise. Medically speaking, a patient can get better; a patient can get worse, then get better; a patient can get worse and then die; a patient can get better, then get worse, then get better, then get worse . . .this can go on for a very long time.

* * *

Story number two. A pretty little girl with red curls once came down with chicken pox. "Better now than when she's older," said the pretty little girl's mother, who also had red curls, and was rather pretty herself, even if her judgment was flawed. The little girl's mother did know enough, however, to give the little girl oatmeal baths, and also warned her against scratching. To pass the time, and keep the little girl's mind off her itching, her mother read her fairy tales. "Sleeping Beauty" was one. You recall how it goes: As foretold by a vengeful fairy, it is the fate of a newborn princess that in her fifteenth year she will prick herself on a spindle and fall down dead. Well, fate is fate, but if one has access to the right interceder, it can sometimes be softened: not dead but, for the next hundred years, sound asleep. Even so, the king banishes all spindles from the kingdom. Nevertheless, in her fifteenth year the princess finds the single spindle overlooked and pricks her finger on it. The rest is history. One hundred years pass by. Prince Charming comes along to rouse the princess, proving (in unexpurgated versions) there's more than one way of being pricked. It's also a scientific fact that unprotected sex has always been risky. Complications can ensue, the same as with chicken pox. Which brings us back to that pretty little girl with red curls who by now has fallen asleep in her bed.

Closing the book, her mother leaned over and kissed the little girl on her forehead. How warm she felt. Feverish, thought the little girl's mother, noticing also for the first time what looked like a faint rash just beneath the girl's skin. She telephoned her pediatrician. He was out of town, so she spoke with the covering doctor.

"Chicken pox is highly contagious. No point bringing her in. Rash and fever are characteristic," he told her. Naturally, he didn't make house calls. Well, what doctor does? Certainly not her regular pediatrician. After hanging up, the mother was still worried. She telephoned the hospital.

"Don't bring her here," she was told. "Chicken pox in children isn't normally serious, but it is highly contagious. We have some very sick patients with already compromised immune systems. For them, chicken pox can be fatal." Unfortunately for the pretty little girl with red curls, chicken pox could also be fatal. The next time her mother looked in on her, the little girl was no longer breathing.

Idiopathic thrombocytopenic purpura, the emergency room resident eventually wrote on her death certificate. "It means she died from a lack of blood platelets," the resident told the little girl's mother, and tried to console her. "It wasn't your fault. There was no way you could know." Well, of course not. She hadn't gone to medical school. She didn't even know the right words; *petechia, purpura, ecchymosis.* If only she had, she could have said them on the telephone, and maybe saved her daughter.

"My little girl died of chicken pox," she said instead, bitterly, ever after. Nor did the pretty little girl's mother ever recover fully herself.

Materia medica: Beside a sleeping child, a woman sits reading. A book of fairy tales lies closed on the floor, and open, in the woman's lap, is a tome on ancient cures. (Before going farther, I probably should mention—both mother and daughter are redheads; also, the little girl has chicken pox.)

First cure: In Ireland it was at one time believed sufficient in the case of childhood disease to have the patient first fast, following which a live trout would be placed into the child's throat. If a trout were not available, a live frog would do. Afterward, the still living animal would be put back into the stream or pond from which it had come. This may in fact be the origin of the expression "a frog in one's throat," used to explain a momentary congestion interfering with speech. On the other hand, it's possible this expression comes instead from an early belief that to dangle a toadlet on a string down one's throat would cure almost any sort of soreness. (By strange coincidence, in the next room is a tadpole the little girl is raising. Naturally, no one is about to try dangling it down her throat. It's neither here nor there in the story. Why even mention it, then?)

Second cure: In the old days, toadlets weren't all that got dangled—not by a long shot. It was also held that for toothache, relief could be had from suspending in one's throat the tooth of a dead horse; or else rubbing the hand of a dead man over one's jaw.

Third cure: While such cures were being practiced in the West, in the East it was believed that the bone of a living person could cure any number of ailments. Popular pharmacopeias from Korea, for instance, relate numerous tales of dutiful daughters who cut off their fingers, cooked them in porridge, then served them to their mothers who were sick, mad in some cases, and affected their cures. That even experienced doctors could not compare with such filial girls was the point of these stories.

The reading woman has stopped reading. Her eyes are now closed, and so is the book. Perhaps she is thinking: Well, if a daughter would do this for a mother, what might a mother not do for a daughter. Cutting out her own heart probably would not seem too much. *Maybe* that's what she's thinking. On the other hand, perhaps she's only considering how limited is the range of what doctors know. This happened not long ago to the woman's nephew—he came down with chicken pox twice.

"But you can't have it twice, can you?" the woman had asked her sister.

"Of course not," said the sister. "The first time it was hives. 'Are you sure it's chicken pox?' I asked his pediatrician that time. 'Are you absolutely positive? Do you think, possibly, it could be an allergic reaction to the antibiotic he's been taking for an ear infection?' 'Oh no,' said the pediatrician. 'It's definitely chicken pox.'"

The sister's husband is a doctor himself: not a pediatrician but still a physician. Naturally, he sided with his fellow practitioner. Well, he sided with him until the next month when the little boy came down with chicken pox again. Then he sided with his wife. "It was hives the first time," he said.

"See, I was right," the woman's sister told her.

"How awful!" the woman replied. "An allergic reaction to medicine can be serious."

"Of course," the sister agreed. "It can be fatal." Well, so can chicken pox. Thinking this, the woman, whose eyes have remained closed all this time, opens them. She glances at the sleeping child. Then she rises suddenly, causing her book of ancient cures to fall to the floor, and reaches for the telephone.

Story number three. "A pretty little girl with red curls once came down with chicken pox," begins the storyteller. "We've heard that story before," some of the listeners grumble.

"Ah, yes; perhaps," says the storyteller, but even so she talks on. Among her audience, eyelids droop and heads nod, but still they listen. They're old enough to know that where a story goes, even a familiar one, is anybody's guess.

"Fortunately, the little girl's mother was persistent," they hear the storyteller say. "She wasn't satisfied just giving oatmeal baths, or good at taking no for an answer. Nor did she believe in telling everything she knew. When she telephoned the hospital, she didn't so much as mention chicken pox.

"'My little girl is black and blue all over,' was what she said. She'd learned the value of exaggeration from her mother. 'Ziebn iss a liegn; seven is a lie,' the little girl's grandmother used to warn. Who knew? Perhaps this was a case of child abuse. 'You'd better bring your little girl in right away,' the woman was instructed. That's what she did. The doctor took one look, then called for blood tests.

"'It's a good thing you brought her when you did. Patients in her condition can bleed to death.' The doctor called for a transfusion of immune globulin and platelets. Almost right away the little girl began to recover. She was sent home one week later, nearly all better. 'But she needs to come back weekly to have her blood tested, at least for a year,' the hematologist told the little girl's mother. See, once a hospital is involved, careful follow-up is called for. It reduces the risk of lawsuit. Which may explain why hospitals are so reluctant to get involved in the first place."

"Is that the end? Did everyone live happily ever after?" call out impatient listeners.

"Almost," says the storyteller. "They lived happily for a long time to come until finally even the little girl was very old. One night she went to bed, died in her sleep, and didn't wake up in the morning. But that's just what came after, a footnote, not the end of the story by a long shot. That same week the little girl spent in the hospital, it was reported in the news that a new vaccine had been approved to prevent chicken pox. Therefore, if that little girl hadn't come down with chicken pox when she did, she would never have come down with it at all."

On hearing this, the audience understands that 'an ounce of prevention is worth a pound of cure' is the saying intended to be illustrated by the story, and also they see the value of persistence. That timing is everything, is the tale that is being handed down.

The Devil and the Missionaries

Once upon a time a husband, who was fond of minding his own business, and his very principled wife lived across the street from a missionary couple. Before settling in Virginia, the missionaries had served for years first in Japan and then in Korea. They were fluent in many languages, having traveled widely, and also had several degrees between them. Nevertheless, and shockingly to the principled wife, many of the beliefs they subscribed to were the same as those held by skinheads and nazis. Nor was this merely the opinion of the principled wife. The missionary husband had a daily radio program to prove it. Carried by a "Christian Station," his calumny focused on Sodomites, evolutionists and, most often, Jews. Included in this latter category were many of the principled woman's relatives, although she considered herself a free thinker and increasingly believed that, when it came to organized religion, the harm done outweighed the good.

Not, she realized, that her status would matter in the least to the missionary, who'd been Johnny-on-the-spot, for instance, when it came to chastising Madeleine Albright, America's first female Secretary of State. Born Jewish in Poland, raised Catholic, she was now a practicing Episcopalian. Some of her relatives had been killed in the Holocaust. Until newly exposed, her earliest history had remained a mystery, unknown or unclaimed.

"Was she ashamed of her Jewishness?" the missionary asked on the air. "Did she think the church was just some port in a storm to turn to for saving?" The principled woman pondered this question. In fact it was exactly what she thought churches promised. *Take up Christ's cross and be saved. He died that we might have eternal life.* Perhaps, as with so many other things, she'd misunderstood. In any event, she did think that being a missionary and an anti-Semite were mutually exclusive. But when she mentioned this to her oldest living relative, an uncle who lived in Florida, he seemed surprised.

"Why would you think that?" he asked. "Doesn't such thinking fly in the face of history?"

Of course that interchange of views occurred only after she knew. She hadn't known all along. Certainly not when they'd bought their present house and moved in, nor for the next several years after. In fact, had she minded her own business, as her husband would have advised, she might not have known it even yet, in which case she could have gone on living as she had been, politely unacquainted with the neighbors.

But somehow the Devil got wind of the situation. Alas, it's not in his nature to let an opportunity to cause mischief pass him by. Naturally, he found the chance to pit a woman of principles against a pair of missionaries irresistible. Therefore, he made sure that the missionaries at last got around to welcoming their no longer new neighbors to the neighborhood by holding a dinner party and inviting them.

Though the principled woman's husband would have preferred staying home, he left the decision up to his wife. She said, "I think it's only right for us to go."

"We should have done this sooner," the missionaries said, making introductions and settling their guests. Small talk commenced, family-centered for the most part and non-controversial. It was then that the principled wife learned the missionary couple had missionary children campaigning for God in faraway places, supervised a mission school serving black children in the heart of D.C., and that he conducted a radio program. She had only time enough to ask, "What time and what station?" and find out, before the food was blessed and served. The menu included fruit punch, chicken and rice, pokeweed salad, and peach cobbler for dessert.

"Pokeweed," said the principled woman. "I've always wanted to taste pokeweed." It was true. Well, at any rate, since she'd first come across mention of it in some country kitchen folklore journal which had gone on to warn that if picked or cooked wrong pokeweed could be poisonous. But as the article provided no further instructions, the principled woman had never tried it. At least until now.

"The trick's in how you cook it," the missionary husband explained, then edifyingly displayed a batch of freshly picked, raw leaves.

"You don't want to eat pokeweed unless it's boiled at least thirty minutes," said the missionary wife. "Don't worry, I always cook mine longer than necessary," she added.

"How delicious," said the principled woman, who conscientiously preferred vegetables to meat. "Have some," she offered her husband, as she took a second helping.

"Thank you, but I'm saving room for dessert," he said, having pushed his own portion to the far side of his plate. His hungry wife ate that too.

"Wasn't dinner fun? Don't they seem like nice people?" she said, going home.

"Ummm," said her husband, noncommittally.

"Well, at least they're not racist," she added. She might have said more, except no sooner had she stepped through the doorway than her intestines convulsed and sent her racing for the nearest bathroom. Flushing repeatedly and uselessly against the noises of her flatulence she wondered if her suffering was caused by stomach poisoning. "Of course not; it was just my first time eating pokeweed that it disagreed with me. Probably I ate too much," she told herself. She might have blamed it on the peach cobbler if her husband's peaceful snores were not already resonating through the house.

By the time morning came the woman felt fine. As she sipped tea and ate buttered toast, she considered the night before and the missionaries. "We'll have to invite them back. It's only right," she told her husband at dinner, and took his silence for assent. In Hell, the Devil overheard her and smiled. He smiled again the next day as the woman made her way across the street and rang the missionaries' doorbell.

"Why, yes," they said. "Dinner next Saturday will be fine. We'll be looking forward to it." Back home, the woman began to plan her menu. She settled on fish for the main course. Hospitable as she was feeling that minute, though, she wanted to do more than just feed them. But what? Then exactly as the Devil knew would happen, she remembered the missionary's radio show. She could listen to it. That's what she could do. How surprised and pleased the missionaries would be when she discoursed on it with them at dinner.

Therefore, the following morning at the scheduled time, the woman tuned her radio to the proper station and turned it on. She listened carefully, then listened carefully again the next morning, and the one after that. "The Sodomites' houses were burned to the ground," she heard her neighbor say approvingly. "Only when the Jews are gone from America will God turn back his face on us." How much better off they all might have been had she only rushed off after the first time and washed out her ears. How could he say such things? He was a widely read and educated person after all. Surely he knew where such talk led. In her head, the woman could hear her mother's voice:

"Germany was full of educated people—scientists, musicians, college professors. They were highly educated and they were nazis." Naturally that was a group for which her mother had no use. Missionaries were another. "When they come, don't open the door. The only thing to do is ignore them," her mother used to advise. Perhaps she was right, the principled woman thought now. The older she got, the more often it seemed to her that her mother was right, about so many things. Too bad her mother was dead and she had no one to say this to. Well, she did have her uncle, and her brother, who lived in New Jersey.

"I don't know what to do. I think I've never been this close to evil before," the principled woman said into the phone. There was a pause. She heard her brother clear his throat.

"Excuse me, but you had dinner in their house?" her brother asked, amazed.

"Well, yes, but that was before I knew they were nazis."

"I realize that," her brother said. "But I mean you actually had dinner at a neighbor's house? I mean we've been living here, what, maybe twenty-five years? and we've never been to any neighbor's house for dinner. I can't even begin to imagine. . ." He interrupted himself to say, "Well, I realize the point is he's an anti-Semite. But still it's strange to think of your having dinner at his house. I mean any neighbor's house."

"Ummm," the principled woman said, and changed the topic. It was clear to her that discussing the matter further with her brother would be useless. Afterward, though, whenever she thought of this conversation, she smiled. But then she thought, too, how her brother often was right, the same as their mother. "You're better off not getting too chummy with neighbors. That way you won't know what they think or have to deal with it." On this point at least, the principled woman's husband and her mother would have agreed.

That evening she raised the subject with her husband. "So, what should we do?" the principled woman asked.

"Do about what?" he replied.

"About the people across the street who are coming to dinner. The ones who don't pay taxes on account of being missionaries, even though they preach a political program—Jews

44

out of America, creationism in the classroom, whom to vote for and whom not. I can hardly believe we actually ate in their house. Do you think the IRS would be interested?"

"In what?" asked her husband.

"Their non-payment of taxes," said the woman.

Her husband sighed. "The thing to do is mind our own business. That way we won't have to worry about bullet holes through our windows, bombs through our front door, crosses burned on our lawn. I don't see why you listen to that program anyway." Born black and Baptist in the deep south, he had more experience than his principled wife when it came to such matters.

"But isn't that what they did in Germany?" she asked.

"We're in America," he said. "I'm thinking only of your well-being."

The woman frowned. Then she asked, "What about dinner? Can I uninvite them?"

"You can do as you like. Why are you asking me now? Had you listened to me earlier, you wouldn't have gotten mixed up with them in the first place. I wasn't the one who wanted to go visiting."

"Well, you didn't say no, did you?" she pointed out.

"I also don't listen to his radio program. Some things I'd rather not know."

The woman could see her husband would be of no help. She told herself, "What's done is done. They'll come here and eat, and then I'll never need to have anything to do with them again." Which turned out truer than the woman knew at the time. In Hell, overhearing her thoughts, once more the Devil smiled. He saw that the principled woman could use his assistance.

Therefore, the next morning, which was also the day of the dinner, the Devil came up into the world, disguised as a fish-monger. "Down home," he told the woman, selling her salmon, "there isn't any side dish we like better than poke-weed. There's nothing matches it for bringing out the flavor of fish."

"Funny you should mention it," said the woman. "Only last week, I ate pokeweed for the first time."

"Good, wasn't it?" said the Devil. "Just the other day, I saw some growing alongside the jogging path. 'Umm, umm, umm,' I said to my wife. 'How long's it been now since we had a good pokeweed salad?' Of course you never want to overcook it."

"Is that so?" said the woman. A runner herself, for reasons of health, she knew just the path the Devil had mentioned. As she paid for the fish she looked thoughtful. Or, perhaps, just a teensy bit less principled than usual. In any event, high noon found her on her hands and her knees, hastily harvesting pokeweed leaves, along with a few stems and some roots. It took her longer than she'd planned.

Back home at last she showered quickly and got dressed. "If I want everything ready on time, I'll have to work fast," she told herself.

First she rinsed off the fish and set it to marinate in a glass dish, along with herbs, aged vinegar and oil. Next she wrapped vegetables in foil to roast. Last of all, she washed her pokeweed carefully and dropped it into a pot of boiling water. Then while everything was cooking the woman went into the dining room to set the table. Meanwhile, her husband poked his head into the kitchen to see if he could lend a hand. Everything seemed under control. Well, he did notice the clock was several minutes slow and fixed it, after which he went off to turn on the outside lights. The last thing he needed was for someone to slip, and to have a lawsuit on his hands.

Back in the kitchen, the woman checked her dinner. She was just turning off the oven when the doorbell rang. She looked at the clock. About time to drain the pokeweed. "You never want to overcook it," the woman told herself, discarding everything in the pot but the leaves. "If someone gets sick at least it won't kill them." This last she truly believed.

"Dinner's delicious," the missionaries said, seated around the table a little while later.

"Thank you," said the woman. "Have some more pokeweed. I fixed it especially for you. I'd have some myself except I'm allergic."

"I'm saving room for dessert, apple pie a la mode," her husband told them.

Not long afterward the missionaries left. "It was a lovely evening, but tomorrow is Sunday. We're always up early for church." But of course the next day they weren't. With twisted intestines and stomachs in turmoil, they'd died in the night and gone straight to the Devil, who was very pleased to have them in Hell.

"Finally, someone who knows how to cook pokeweed," he said. Even so, he sent a minor demon to supervise them. "You never want to overcook it," the Devil told him. Therefore, the missionaries were always having to sample it before it was ready. And if in Hell you can't die again, it did keep them running. Seated on his throne, the Devil smiled. There is nothing he enjoys better than a good scatological joke.

Sometime later, in a book she was reading, the principled wife was surprised to come across this about pokeweed: The poison's strongest in the stems and roots. You want to pick only new shoots. So much for the missionaries' cooking instructions, she told herself, and felt more principled than she had for some time. She read the poison part aloud to her husband.

"Yes, I know," he said. "My mother used to fix it."

"Your mother? Why didn't you tell me?" asked his wife.

Her husband shrugged. "You never asked," he said. And that was that. Oh, yes. They did live happily for a long time to come. And if the wife never cooked pokeweed again, why would she?

"There's no one we know anymore that eats it," she said.

Claudia

Claudia, oh best beloved child; first and last, my older, only sister, whose presence intrudes, always, in my life, in my dreams, in my thoughts. My saying so implies no criticism, far from it, not, for instance, as if I were to accuse her of obtrusion, "ob" implying opposite, against, as in opposed to, or opponent. I mean only to convey a neutral imperative, that Claudia's presence is with me always, my knowledge of her a permanent fixture in my life, my life without her, to me, unimaginable. That much is fact, beyond dispute, incontrovertible.

Why then is it so difficult for me to describe her, to say what she's like? Why is it, whenever I try, I find I am lacking a template, and her pattern eludes me?

Well, I think, sisters after all. Whatever one sister says is only half of the story. Tales recounted by sisters are often at variance, told at different frequencies that are sometimes discordant. I search out stories of sisters, and save them. Some of them are also dreams.

First story: Two sisters; the older one is often in trouble of one sort or another. The younger one, frequently, feels called upon to stop what she is doing, interrupt her life, attend to the older one's needs. Just as the younger sister is about to begin graduate school, a crucial stage in her life, one that has required careful planning and consideration, her sister disappears; becomes, officially, a missing person. The police are not that interested. They have many such cases. Hers is only one more. The younger sister feels she has no choice in the matter. She delays her college plans, puts her own life on hold, and goes in search of her sister. One night she has this dream: She is wandering the byways of some big city, she thinks it is Chicago, calling out her sister's name. Then, in some dark alley, or half-lit street, she finds her. The sister has become a homeless person, shoeless and in rags; also, her head is missing. She is a homeless, headless person. Even so, the younger sister knows her right away. She wants to help. But the older sister tells her, "Don't worry about me. Get on with your life. I can take care of myself."

Second story: Two sisters; the younger one is a disorganized person. Her room, her possessions, are never in order. Her mother and her older sister endlessly scold her, trying to get her to organize her life better, straighten her room, put her closets and drawers in order. One night she dreams that she has died. Her sister and mother, both in real life and in her dream, are in Europe at the time. She dreams that after she is dead they both come home from Europe and begin to organize her things. They straighten her room, go through her closets, clean out her drawers. They are happy she is dead. Now, finally, everything is neat, and all her possessions are in place.

Third story: Two sisters; the younger one is me. I dream that I'm a famous artist, a sculptor. I specialize in heads; some of them are self-portraits. My work is acclaimed by art critics. Their commentary calls attention to the frequency with which I use my sister as a model. Only I, the artist, can't see it. However carefully I look, or long I stare, the figures look like me. I tell my dream to a friend who is a painter herself. She seems fascinated and keeps on talking about it. "It's only a dream," I say finally. "It isn't real life." "Sure, a dream," she says, "but it came out of your head."

This is not a dream, not a story. It is a memory. "Why don't you leave, go away? No one wants you here." Claudia is perhaps five when she starts telling me this. I would have been three. Perhaps she told it to me sooner. If so, I don't remember. Our earliest memories, I have read, begin at age three. "How do you know?" I must have asked her that. I would not just have taken her word for it. She is glad, more than glad, to tell me. She has overheard our parents talking late at night, whispering in bed, sighing to each other, discussing me. It seems they are stuck. Possession is nine-tenths of the law. I am here, in their house. No other relative can be found who is willing to take me. Gently, even affectionately, Claudia hints there might be alternatives. "You could run away," she suggests, "disappear."

Maybe there are many older siblings who have told younger children the same thing, but I have only ever heard of one other case. A woman I used to work with told me about her two children. Her son was the older and also her favorite. She actually told me this. "A boy," she said, "especially when he's the first child, always will have a special place in his mother's heart. The younger one, the girl, will always know it. That is why a younger girl always carries inside herself a special sadness." This woman's son used to tell his sister the same things Claudia told me. "They don't really love you," he said. "They wish they could give you back. They're sorry now they ever took you in the first place. But it's too late. No one else will have you." The sister was about to be married when she told her mother for the first time what the brother used to say to her when they were children. "Why didn't you tell me?" the mother asked. "Why didn't you come to me and ask for the facts?" "I was afraid," the girl told her. "I couldn't take the chance of finding out that what he said was true." I, too, have always been unwilling to take such a chance.

Claudia was a remarkable infant, according to our mother's version of the story. She was almost, maybe even actually, of genius caliber. She crawled on the day that they took her home from the hospital. On the other hand, isn't it also possible that, tormented by gas, she only pulled herself across the mattress? Anything is possible. Our mother insists on Claudia's absolute precociousness. She did everything early, until I came along. After I was born, Claudia began losing ground. Our mother believes that Claudia's grief was so great at finding herself no longer an only child that it sapped her of the ability to concentrate. Gradually, she became like everybody else, the same as other people's children. Our mother has always held onto her belief, however, that deep within, Claudia retains the capacity to be exceptional.

Claudia has told me that she believes our mother's faith in her, in her abilities, was not in her own best interests. It made her nervous and apprehensive. Too much was expected of her. It is true that Claudia was a nervous child, perpetually worried. That much is obvious even in snapshots of her from that time. In most of them I, too, am present. Claudia, nearly always, is in the foreground, and I am somewhere behind her. Often, she can be seen looking back over her shoulder, as if fearful of being overtaken. But even when she is looking directly at the camera, she seems distracted, anxious, as though it's taking all her effort just to keep her eyes from focusing elsewhere. She is clearly a child with problems on her mind. Only in her baby pictures, taken before I was born, does Claudia seem at ease and unworried.

I take out other photographs and look at them. My husband Vergil has an older sister. Her two daughters are several years apart. In all the pictures that we have of them, Honore, the elder one, appears preoccupied. It is only in her baby pictures, taken before Hilary was born, that she is seen laughing, her expression unconcerned. Can it be only a coincidence? Or do all older siblings actually bear scars derived from early knowledge of displacement? I cannot test my theory on snapshots of Vergil and his sister. Their house burned to the ground, with everything in it, when they were in their teens. There are no photographs of them from before that time.

Several years ago, Claudia told me about a conversation she'd had with her husband, Gerald. "Doesn't it ever occur to you that your mother might be wrong?" he'd asked her. "Don't you think if you were capable of doing more, by now you would have done so?" She said that instead of making her feel downcast, his words had the opposite effect. It was as though he had released her to be no more than herself. "I felt a great sense of relief," she told me. "Finally I could relax. I didn't have to try so hard all of the time."

I am of two minds about Gerald's advice. Naturally, I am pleased to see that Claudia is happier, more at ease with herself. On the other hand, I also believe that just because our mother's assessment was wrong, that doesn't mean Claudia lacks talent altogether. For instance, Claudia writes stories and poems, fragments of stories and poems, and sends them to me. I write for a living. She wants my professional opinion. I tell her that I think they're wonderful, which is the truth, but I know she doesn't always, or even often, believe me. I think if Claudia would ever finish the stories she begins, and send them to magazines, they would be published. Despite my prodding, however, she won't. I never say to her, though, what I truly believe, that she isn't living up to her potential. If I were to tell her that, it would only upset her and also I would wind up sounding the same as our mother.

Stories, dreams, memories, and photographs; what other ways have we to recollect, or reconstruct, our early lives? Yet how reliable are these? When I try picturing Claudia as a child, this is the picture I see: Claudia standing in front of the mirror. Long, thick, richly colored hair. Our mother standing behind her, brushing, braiding, affixing brightly colored barrettes. This is the morning ritual in our house. Every morning. When it is finished, our mother steps back and admires her work. Sometimes, often, almost always, she reaches out and, lovingly, pats Claudia on her head. I, too, want long hair, but my mother says no. "Your hair is too thin, too straight, too flyaway," she tells me. Once a month she takes me to Best & Co. and instructs whoever is there to cut off as much of my hair as has grown in since the last time.

This is not the picture that Claudia sees. The scene that she remembers she weaves into a story, and sends to me. As usual, the story is unfinished, not yet complete. It is about Erin, a young girl with long, thick, chestnut-colored hair. She wants to wear it down, loose, around her shoulders, like a princess. Her mother will not let her, not even for a party. Every day, the mother insists on braiding Erin's hair. She stands behind the little girl, yanking, twisting, pulling her head this way and that, making parts that remind Erin of anthills, and plaits that Erin knows are also called pigtails and are, in any event, in her case pulled so tightly as to make her scalp actually tingle. Erin dreads having her hair brushed.

Claudia and I both can remember wanting to be Catholic when we were growing up, but not for the same reasons, nor with the same degree of intensity. There was a Catholic school across the street from where we lived. We could see it from our bedroom window. If boys as well as girls attended it, I don't recall them. Boys had nothing to do with my life at that time; for all the thought I gave them, they could have been a different species altogether. The Catholic girls were another matter. We watched them every chance we got as they played in their schoolyard. They looked different from us. They were paler and neater; however hard they played, their blouses stayed tucked in their skirts and their faces looked scrubbed. I admired everything about them, but especially their freckles and noses, small and turned up. Also, the games that they played seemed more interesting than ours. That was why I wanted to be Catholic. I informed my mother. "I want to jump rope Double Dutch, the way they do," I told her.

"You don't have to be Catholic for that." My mother laughed at me. "There's nothing to it. I used to do it." I begged her to show me how. "You can't jump rope in an apartment," she said. "The crackpots would complain." She meant the couple from Holland who lived beneath us. They had a brown dog named Cocoa. For a brief period of time I actually thought that crackpot was just another word for Dutch. The only time I can remember them complaining was when Claudia and I let the bathtub overflow on purpose so we could play "Maid of the Mist," having been to Niagara Falls with our parents the summer before. My mother promised that when we moved to our own house in Queens she'd get me a jump rope and teach me how to use it. She also promised we could have a dog. We learned in this way that a promise is not the same thing as a binding agreement.

Claudia's reason for wanting to be Catholic was different from mine. She wanted to have a confirmation, wear a white dress, stand up in church with her hair unbraided, loose around her shoulders, like royalty. "You don't have to be Catholic to wear a white dress," our mother told her. "When you get married, you can wear one then." The way things turned out, though, Claudia didn't. "Elope," our mother told us with increasing frequency as we got older. "It's much better than a wedding, and cheaper." Weddings, she said, were a waste of money. She'd never had one, and we didn't either.

One thing I don't know is this: Did Claudia's enthusiasm for the Catholic religion actually go beyond confirmation? Was all of her talk about a white dress just her way of sublimating what she was really after?

* * *

I receive in the mail from her a new version of the story about Erin, the girl with the long, chestnut-colored hair. Erin now wants to be Catholic. Her parents claim to be Ethical Culturists themselves. So did ours. In fact, though, both sets of parents are Jewish.

"God is everywhere," Erin's mother tells her. "Church itself is immaterial." If God is everywhere, Erin sets out to find Him. She looks under beds, behind the stove, inside closets. Of course He isn't there. She should have known better, she tells herself. Besides, why should she even care about so sneaky and elusive a God as this one. Erin knows what she wants, who she cares for. It is the Virgin Mary whom Erin loves, with her gentle smile and downcast eyes, who cradles baby Jesus always in her arms. Erin knows where to find her, too, anytime she wants. Mary stands patiently, just where you'd expect her to be, on the steps of the Sacred Heart Church on the corner. How smart she is, Erin thinks, how clever. Hadn't she figured out a way to give birth to a wonderful child, the Lord himself, without having to participate in so appalling an act as sexual intercourse?

Erin is not alone in her thinking. The author Rumer Godden wrote in her autobiography that well into her teens she included the following in her nightly prayer: "Please God let me grow up good enough to be like the Virgin Mary and have a baby without being married."

Marriage of course wasn't the point. Sex was. Here is another writer recalling her early education. An older cousin explained to her how women get babies. The writer, hearing it for the first time, froze. She went into shock. She didn't believe it. "It's true all right," the older cousin said. "My mother told me. Everybody has to do it to start a baby." The informer paused. "Except for my mother." Ah! thought the writer. She was ten at the time and knew how to reason. One statement could be true, or the other, but not both. She questioned the cousin. "If everybody has to, why not your mother?" Her cousin was glad to explain: Every night, night after night, her mother said to her father, "Not tonight, Lenny. Maybe tomorrow." She kept putting it off and putting it off until, finally, she'd put it off for so long that the cousin was already born and the mother didn't have to do it.

Erin's first experience with sex education leaves her with feelings similar to that writer's. She doesn't hear about sex from a cousin, though. Erin's mother, as ours, writes away for pamphlets from companies that manufacture sanitary napkins. When Erin reads them her child's body turns rigid, almost catatonic. Later, just thinking about them, in school during spelling for instance, she grows pale; at lunchtime she's unable to eat. My own mother, she thinks, actually gave me those pamphlets. She must have read them herself, considered them good. Erin has dreams about love. Her mother's pamphlets discuss mucous secretions. Erin begins to hate her mother, hate all grown-ups with their endless talk about cleanliness, and fresh underwear, washing your hands, using a nail brush. If this is what Erin's mother, what all grown-ups, are up to all the time, no wonder they have to bathe, and change their underwear, so often.

Well, fiction after all. It could mean anything. Even memories are more reliable. I think of Clarissa, our other sister, born prematurely and less than a year old when she died. I remember how she looked when they brought her home from the hospital. She was tiny, wrinkled, and bright red. This was not the sister for whom Claudia and I had often begged. Clarissa had a nurse to take care of her, Miss Wilkinson, who wore a white uniform and was English. Claudia added her to the growing list of adults she didn't like. Loathe was a new word between us. "I loathe Miss Wilkinson," Claudia said, and giggled. The first time she said it, I was surprised, thinking she had said love. "Not love, loathe," she corrected me.

"Me too," I said, anxious for Claudia's approval. "I loathe her, too." I was ten at the time.

When I try recalling, now, how I felt about my mother's

pregnancy, I can't recall a thing. The obliviousness with which, apparently, I regarded her condition, surprises even me. Could it be a matter of repression? Delayed development of normal observational skills? An early propensity for ignoring what was inconvenient? Or did I simply have other matters on my mind?

A woman I know who was twelve when her mother was pregnant with her youngest sister tells me how she felt. "I hated going anywhere with my mother. Everyone could tell just by looking at her that she was pregnant. All of them knew what my mother had done, what she still might do. It was the most humiliating time of my life."

Claudia, too, was twelve when our mother was pregnant. If she felt that same way, she never discussed it with me. Nevertheless, Clarissa's birth marked a turning point in our lives. It wasn't long after when we moved to the suburbs. Claudia, almost overnight, or so it seemed to me, became grown up. She had always been tall for her age. Now she stopped growing. Her breasts came in. That was how I thought of it at the time. Because she was otherwise so slender, with narrow shoulders and hips, the enormousness of her breasts was all the more noticeable. Eyes followed them, wherever she went; boy's eyes definitely, but even girls stared. I myself found it difficult in her presence to look elsewhere. Eventually, and I believe as a direct result of trying to deal both with her newly developing body and with the attention it engendered, Claudia began to walk with a special gait. She held herself carefully and stepped gingerly as though afraid she might otherwise disturb her precarious equilibrium.

Though it seems obvious to me now that Claudia's sudden maturity would have required at least some emotional adjustment on her part, at the time I didn't see it. I thought that Claudia was blessed in every way. I realized, of course, that age was a factor. Therefore, I was willing to take a back seat, temporarily. I stuffed her bras with socks and cotton balls and tried them on. I waited patiently for that day, or week or month or year, when my own breasts would come in.

* * *

Here is a photograph of me at age thirteen. I am leaning against a tree. I'm barefoot, dressed in dungarees and an over-size man's shirt that may have belonged to my father. Bangs cover my forehead and part of my eyes. It is hard to under-stand how I can see. Except for hair that hangs down to my waist, I could be mistaken for a boy. My body is no different now from when I was age ten. Only recently, though, have I given up eating. I am anorexic, but we don't call it that. No one we know knows the word yet.

"She lives on air," my mother says. "I was like that when I was her age." Do I hear in her voice, for the first time, that we may have something in common? Or do I just imagine it? Beyond that brief recognition, however, no further attention is paid to signs that something may be wrong with me. When I get down to eighty-five pounds, the neighbors start to notice. My mother assures them it's just a stage I'm going through. "She only does it for attention." She tells them that the best thing is simply to ignore it. Both my parents ignore it and, eventually, on my own, I begin eating again. "See, didn't I say all along she'd outgrow it?" my mother says, and it does seem that, at least in my case, my mother's cure was effective.

Although anorexia is now a well-known term for a wide-spread eating disorder, thought to be neurotic in origin, I believe at the time the only thing on my mind was an over-whelming desire for thinness. If I could not have breasts like Claudia's, look as she did, I might as well strike out in new directions. As casual as I may appear in the photograph to a disinterested observer, I had a goal. It was to be rail thin and look like Cher, the teen-age singer of popular ballads who has since filled out and grown famous. Perhaps she, too, would have preferred all along having a figure like Claudia's.

Only after giving birth to Zina, during the time I nursed her, was my body ever like that. I walked up and down the hospital corridor then in my transparent nightgown, stepping gingerly, carefully, my milk-full breasts swaying slightly. A nurse told me to put on a robe. "It's cold in the corridor," she said. "Also anyone can see through that gown." As if I cared. As if I wouldn't have been pleased for the whole world to see what I finally had.

I nursed Zina for months. The fierceness of my love for her amazed me, but even had I loved her less, I think I would have gladly nursed forever just to keep my breasts.

"Nursing is so primitive," Claudia told me. Her son, Eliot, was bottle-fed. "Formula," she said, "is sanitary, scientific, modern."

Long before that, though, still in our teens, we already were moving in different directions. By the time my hair was long Claudia's was short. Though our mother had protested at first, in the end she went along, accompanying Claudia to the beauty parlor and even paying for a "styling." Afterward, Claudia had bleached her hair, at home, in the sink, using peroxide from a brown plastic bottle. She sat outside in the sun so it would "take better." The resulting color, presumably, was some shade of blonde. Claudia set her hair, nightly, on wide metal rollers, then slept on them. Every morning she teased her hair, with a special comb, until it stuck almost straight out. She spent hours at a time in front of the mirror in the only bathroom in the house, plastering her face with pancake make-up and applying thick strokes of bright colored, often orange, lipstick to her mouth. She dressed in sweaters and straight-cut tight skirts. She wore panty girdles, hose and pointy-toed shoes with spiked heels. When she walked in them she wobbled. She cut classes and went to Forty-second Street with friends who dressed as she did, to pick up sailors.

When we brought home report cards it was no surprise to me that Claudia was failing, everything. I believe that for several semesters in a row the highest grade that she received was in the fifties. This was in a school where just showing up was usually sufficient to pass any class. My grades were all in the nineties though I didn't so much as open a textbook at home to study. The reading I did was rarely for school. I read novels by such writers as Jack London, F. Scott Fitzgerald,

Hemingway. Now and then I read plays—Bernard Shaw, Henrik Ibsen. I read every book in our house. I read non-fiction, too, books I sneaked out of the public library, then sneaked back in again: *I Was a Teenage Dope Addict, Love Without Fear, The Opium Eater.* I read women's magazines my mother bought. I was grown up before I wondered at her taste in reading. There was a column in one on marital problems that I found of particular interest. Every month it offered a new case history:

"John and Muriel sit nervously in the counselor's waiting room. Embarrassed and uncertain, this is their last hope for a resolution to their marital crisis. Their four-year relationship has been troubled almost from the start by Muriel's reluctance concerning sex and John's inability to communicate to her what pleases him."

Once Muriel and John are in the counselor's office, readers learn that she was a virgin when they married and he was not. "At first he found her shyness appealing, but as their relationship matured, it became clear to them both that their sexual interaction was a source of mutual dissatisfaction." By the end of every article, both partners were always on their way to fuller, better lives. The key was communication.

"Overcoming the sexual problem was great," Muriel says, "but just as important was that we learned so much about ourselves." I read these stories as fairy tales. The characters in them were far removed from my life. I knew no one at all who was like them.

At home nobody said a word to Claudia or me, either about our appearance or her behavior, and certainly not about our grades in school, or choice of reading. I didn't discuss my reading even with Claudia. She was hardly ever home to talk with. Also, she had given up books completely, though not permanently. Sometimes she read movie magazines, or "true romances."

What I do not understand, to this day, is how our parents could have paid so little attention. When Claudia and I, sometimes, discuss it now the only possibility we see, I do not call it an explanation, is that when they were our ages our parents were already on their own. According to their stories, they earned their livings, helped support their families, and sent themselves to college. When Vergil asks me how, though, I have no answer. Even so, I think perhaps they just didn't see what could be done with grown-up children who behaved as we did.

Claudia and I went our separate ways for the rest of our adolescence, almost as though we were no longer sisters. Sometimes people asked us, "Are you two *really* sisters? You don't look anything alike."

"Twins," I'd answer. "We're actually twins. I know we look totally different, but with fraternal twins it's often that way." Naturally, no one believed me. Claudia, when she thought she was out of my hearing, would say, "Sisters? How can you ask that? We're hardly even related." There were people who knew us who believed that at least one or the other of us was an orphan, or adopted, or both.

Childhood memories: They can be as familiar as a bad dream; they can sometimes point the way toward enlightenment. I see clearly now what I have missed before. In the stories and poems that Claudia writes and sends me, there are never any sisters. It is almost as though she has never heard of such a relationship, as though sisterhood is inconceivable to her. Sisters are present in everything I write, even just in essays and talks that I give. Sometimes they are central to my theme; other times they can barely be glimpsed, lurking as they do in the background; but, always, they are there. No wonder, then, that Claudia's writing is forever fragmented. It's clear to me what she must do. Before she can complete her work, she'll need to add a sister.

The Interpretation of Dreams

My sister Claudia is no longer Jewish, but neither is she Catholic as she once planned. There was a long stretch in her life, say from her late twenties to her mid-thirties, when anytime the subject of religion came up between us, she'd tell me of her involvement in some new one. Now, though, and for some years, she has settled on Presbyterian.

This is how I found out. She telephoned and said, "I was accepted into the church last Sunday."

First, I had to ask, "Which church?" Then I congratulated her. "Was there a ceremony? Did you have a party? Should I send a present?"

"There wasn't any formal ceremony," she said. "I only stood up in church before the congregation and said I accepted Jesus Christ as my Lord and Savior. Well, you have to say that, or they won't let you in. Afterward, everyone came up, shook my hand and said 'congratulations.'"

We seldom discuss religion anymore, but I know that Claudia takes hers seriously. When I forget and telephone her on a Sunday, for instance, she is rarely home. "She's at church," whoever answers will tell me. Intermittently, she has served as a deacon. Nevertheless, despite her conversion and her participation, she cannot escape her past entirely. For one thing, there is Eliot, her son; and also her husband, Gerald, who was raised by religious parents in the Orthodox Jewish tradition.

Gerald's parents took it as a matter of course that when Eliot was eight days old there would be a bris, a religious circumcision ceremony. Neither Claudia nor I had ever attended one before; nor, for that matter, have I been to one since. It was held at Claudia's house. The surgery was performed by a mohel, a religious expert in the matter. Eliot was placed on his back on a T-shaped wooden board to which his arms and legs were bound securely with soft ties. A white handkerchief was soaked in wine, then held to Eliot's mouth for him to suck on, which he did. The board was positioned in my father's lap, and the mohel made the cut. It was over so quickly, one could almost believe nothing had happened. Afterward, there was a party. Not counting Gerald's parents, and perhaps Gerald also, the rest of us could as well have been observing any foreign ritual. What took me by surprise the most that day, however, was the degree of closeness that I felt toward Eliot. I had not anticipated the level of responsibility entailed in the relationship of aunt toward nephew. Whether Claudia feels a similar connection with Zina, my daughter, I have no idea.

Despite Gerald's upbringing, once he left his parents' home he was no longer religious. After both his parents died he gave up its practice almost entirely. Still, he goes to synagogue occasionally, and Eliot sometimes joins him. Now and then Eliot also goes to church with Claudia.

"What does Eliot consider himself?" I once asked Claudia.

"I'm not sure. I think he's confused," she said. "He likes the Jewish religion, and attending services with Gerald, but when he does he misses the pageantry of the church. He likes Christianity, too, but I think he can't quite bring himself to believe in the miracles." I wasn't surprised.

Less than six months after his circumcision Eliot played the part of baby Jesus in the Christmas pageant at Claudia's church, whichever one she was going to at the time. It was easy to see why he'd been chosen. Eliot was a beautiful child, with skin like alabaster, pale blond curls and enormous blue-gray eyes. He was also very good. "He slept through the entire performance," Claudia happily reported some days later.

His behavior worried our mother. "He's a bit placid for a baby," she said. She also thought he was too pale, and fragile looking. "You need to feed him more," she told Claudia. But Claudia didn't.

"Most babies are overfed," Claudia told our mother, having read this in some book. She herself preferred thin babies. Therefore, at the first sign Eliot gave of losing interest in his bottle, Claudia always removed it. Had Claudia not otherwise been such a nurturing parent, I might have shared my mother's concern.

"Don't worry," I told her. "Eliot takes after his father." I meant in appearance, having seen baby photographs of Gerald. However, it turned out to be the truth in more than one way. Both Eliot and Gerald, for instance, are myopic and wear thick-lensed, metal-rimmed eye glasses. They are also both clumsy, which may be a function of their limited vision. Certainly neither condition is cause for alarm. But when Eliot was still quite young, his slow development of motor skills did seem a valid reason for apprehension. Claudia borrowed books from the library on developmental delays in children. "Poor coordination," she read, "sometimes indicates trouble ahead in other areas." She discussed it with Gerald. They were both prepared to be accepting parents. "A slow person can still have a very good life," Claudia said more than once in my hearing. "Especially, someone with as good a disposition as Eliot's," she generally added.

By the time Eliot was in third grade, though, he'd more or less come into his own, although he still seemed lacking in normal motor skills. Claudia was called to his school and told that he was "gifted." This assessment was based on his standardized test scores, which were extraordinarily high. Claudia telephoned to tell me. "I guess he takes after his father," she said. Gerald is a college professor. Of course it came as good news to them both. Claudia borrowed books from the library, and read portions of them to Gerald. They both took seriously their new roles as parents of a gifted child.

Who knows? Certainly Eliot was unusual. He took life in stages. He had a wide range of disparate interests. Each was intensely pursued and was, while it lasted, all that he talked about. Some that I remember were: music, chess, mathematics, history, writing, geology, astronomy, science fiction. "I'm an aspiring historian," he said. "I'm an aspiring geologist." "I'm an aspiring writer." His conversation drove my mother crazy.

"Why doesn't he play baseball, or have a girlfriend, like normal boys his age?" she'd say, complaining.

Claudia, though, took everything he did in her stride. She never criticized him. "He isn't like other children," she told our mother. "He's very sensitive, and intellectually gifted. Once he finds his life's work, he'll settle down to it. Probably he'll be famous."

That's what Claudia said until Eliot got to high school and found religion. He pursued it with the same intensity and earnest sense of purpose that had marked his earlier interests. He was open-minded at first, and ecumenically impartial. "I'm an aspiring theologian," he said. Though this was not the life's work Claudia had in mind for him, all she said at the time was, "I'm sure it's just a stage. He'll outgrow it." In Eliot's senior year, though, Claudia finally lost patience.

Eliot's conversation was all about Judaism, its history and customs. "I'm a Zionist now," he said to anyone listening. He was actively involved in the local chapter of some national association.

"Can you understand it, Mirra?" Claudia asked me. "A person like Eliot, intellectually gifted, with all his advantages, deliberately choosing to run around with a bunch of fanatics." She sent me a paper he'd written for English class.

Redemption
By Eliot Gerstein

At the edge of a small village in Germany just before the start of the Second World War, there lived a young boy with his mother and his father. The boy's mother was Jewish by birth, but his father was not. The nazis at that time were still willing to overlook half-Jewish children of non-Jewish fathers, provided the mothers turned themselves into the authorities, and also provided the children had not been raised in the Jewish religion. Such was the case of the boy in this story. His mother in fact had converted to Christianity herself shortly after the boy had been born. Now the mother said to the father, I will turn myself in.

At first, her husband would not hear of it. No, he said. I cannot allow it. But the woman said, if I do not do this, then we all three will perish, and she gave him no peace until at last he consented. It is not right, he said to himself, and yet, in the end, he went along with her plan.

After the boy's mother had been gone for some months, the nazis updated their policy. Now half-Jewish children of Aryan fathers were to be turned over to the authorities, in return for which the nazis were willing to overlook the original transgression of the fathers. The boy said to his father, I will turn myself in.

At first the father would not hear of it. No, he said. I cannot allow it. But the boy said, if I do not do this, then both of us will perish. And besides, how can I do less than my mother? The boy gave his father no peace, until at last he consented. It is not right, the father said to himself, and yet, in the end, he went along with the plan. Having said yes the first time, a person will find it ever harder to say no.

Early the following morning, the boy bid his father good-bye, and walked to the center of the village where he joined the others. At some point during that day they were all loaded onto trucks and driven north, perhaps a dozen kilometers, to where the forest began. There they left the trucks and began to walk, maybe an hour, maybe more, until they came to a clearing surrounded by trees. They were handed shovels, all except for the youngest children, and told to start digging. When they had dug a large enough ditch, the Germans ordered them to put down their shovels, remove all their clothing, fold it neatly and lay it on the ground. Any jewelry they had with them was to be placed on top of the clothing.

The boy began to undress. Shots rang out, and bodies started falling into the freshly dug pit. That was when the boy began screaming. "You have made a mistake. I am not a Jew," he shouted at the guards. "There has been some error." By this time, he had removed his trousers and was almost out of his underwear. With one hand, he was holding out his penis, and with his other he was pointing at it. "Look! See for yourselves!" He was shrieking. He wanted them to see he was uncircumcised. But when he had done all this, when he stood there naked before them, it turned out he was wrong. He had in fact been circumcised eight days after he was born. Such a thing to forget, he must have thought as he fell headlong into the grave he'd helped to dig.

Eliot had gotten an "A" on his paper. I telephoned Claudia after I read it. "It's well written," I told her.

"Thank you, Mirra, but I wasn't asking for your professional opinion," she said. "The point is, why would a normal person write something like that?"

"Did you ask him?" I asked her.

"He said it was his 'heritage.' What heritage? We're living in America. It's not like Germany or Poland here. In America a person can be anything he likes. Why doesn't Eliot choose something popular?"

I didn't mention to her the matter of history. Nor did I point out how many times I've heard some person say about this or that one: We have a Jewish woman in our church. Or a Jewish man. A woman I once worked with told me, "When I was growing up in Flint, Michigan, my best friend was Jewish. We were both confirmed together."

Claudia and I had had this conversation before. I didn't pursue it.

The next time I saw Eliot he told me, "I'm thinking of becoming a rabbi." It was the summer before he went away to college.

"Really?" I said, surprised. Politics, after all, is one thing. Religion is another. "Doesn't a rabbi have to be very religious?" I asked. I really meant, doesn't it require some sort of a spiritual calling. Surely it couldn't be as simple as just choosing a major. Eliot had never even been Bar Mitzvahed. "Don't rabbis have to believe a lot?"

"A reform rabbi," Eliot replied. "I could believe that much. Besides, you don't actually think they believe everything they say, do you?" I did actually. I let the subject drop.

Several days or perhaps a week later, I dreamed about Eliot. I saw him, in my dream, running down a street; a Christian Zionist in rabbinical robes. He was being chased by a mob of fanatics. How it would have ended, I don't know. Vergil woke me. "You were shouting in your sleep," he said. "Now there's a tear." He wiped it.

Perhaps I should mention here, except for Vergil's marrying me, Judaism has little to do with his life. Also, Vergil is black—African American in some circles, the younger generation of this family, for instance. Still, I often think ancestral memories have given us something extra in common.

Therefore, the following morning I asked him a question I'd wondered about before, "Tell me, do you ever dream about slavery? Do you see yourself on some plantation, or on an auction block, being sold or beaten?"

"No," he answered.

"Well, what *do* you dream, then? Tell me a nightmare."

"Sometimes, I dream that I'm a child again. Grown men are chasing me, swinging bats and chains." He doesn't say the men are white, but that is understood.

"Yes?" I said. "Then what?"

"That's it."

"But do they ever catch you?" I asked. "How does it end?"

"In my sleep I tell myself, 'Hey, it's only a dream. You don't have to put up with this.' Then I wake up."

It sounded good to me, until I remembered how many times I'd been awakened by Vergil's kicking in his sleep. Ah, I thought, *sometimes* you wake up. But other times, just like the rest of us, if you want to get away you have to keep on running. But when I mentioned this later to Vergil he only asked, "Keep on running where? How do you know that I'm not taking a stand? Probably I'm fighting back the enemy."

I considered this a while, trying to decide. I suppose anything is possible. That's always the problem when it comes to interpreting dreams. There's no way to know which parts can be trusted.

Family History

When did I first hear about the Holocaust? How old was I when I knew? I have asked myself that question. I could not have been born knowing—though it sometimes seems that way to me.

I remember this. Perhaps I'm three years old, or four. We are not supposed to tell people that we're Jewish. Which people? Any people. Being Jewish is a secret. Not secret, our mother says. It just isn't anybody's business. Religion, she tells us, is not a subject to discuss. Well, four after all; with whom would I discuss it? And yet, year after year, the subject comes up. "What do you girls want for Christmas?" the neighbors start asking, weeks before Thanksgiving Day. Not just the neighbors. Customers in our father's drugstore want to know, too. "Tell them anything," our mother advises. "We're Jewish," we tell them. "We don't have Christmas." "Anything but that," our father says. He seems put out by our lack of imagination. We try harder. "A horse," I say, and I don't mean just one. "I want a carousel with hordes of painted horses." "She means herds," my sister Claudia explains, who wants the same thing every year: a Christmas tree with colored lights. "Well, a Christmas tree," the grown-ups say. "That's nothing." "Nothing to them," Claudia tells me. Night after night, she dreams that she is putting up her tree and decorating it with ornaments. "Just as I am almost finished, reaching out to fasten down the star, that's when I wake up," she says. One year, our father actually brings home a tree; the same one that stands, year after year, in the window of his store, from November until New Year's Day. When Claudia sees it, standing in our living room, she bursts into tears. "It's too late. Don't you know anything?" she asks weeping. "I don't need a Christmas tree in January." A few days later, the tree is taken down. We don't ever discuss it. It is, almost, as though there had never been a tree in the house.

When I am six, or maybe I'm seven, I hear somehow that Sydney Green was never circumcised. I think I do not even know, at the time, what circumcised means, but I know, as if by osmosis, why Sydney Green wasn't. In case it ever happens again. If America, or even just New York, is ever overrun by nazis, Sydney Green will be safe; he will look the same as everybody.

"As though that would make a difference to nazis," our mother says, her tone ridiculing the very idea. "Hitler didn't care. If you had one Jewish relative, dead or alive, it was sufficient." "Yes?" Claudia asks. "But how did he know?" Our mother frowns at her. "Believe me," she says, "There is always someone who is only too glad to turn someone else in." We believe her.

In Sidney Green's case, of course, his mother was mistaken. In America, everyone is circumcised. Well, not everyone. My husband, Vergil, for instance, is not. I blame that on where he was born—rural Mississippi after all. Vergil also is black, but I believe that has little bearing on the matter. The point is, that circumcision is probably the most commonly performed surgery in this country. In terms of Sidney Green's future, however, his mother's decision is irrelevant. The history of his family is a sad one:

Through a strange mishap of fate, Sidney dies young, struck

by lightning while closing a metal sashed window in a thunder storm. His sister, Sheila, survives him only briefly; then, on her way to meet her father for dinner, she is run over and killed when a car jumps the curb where she is standing, waiting for the light to turn green. When her father hears what has happened, he collapses. He dies in the hospital the following day of heart failure. Not long after, the mother discovers a lump in each breast which, upon examination, turns out to be cancer. She undergoes radiation therapy, incurring severe, disabling, and painful burns when the machine that is treating her goes haywire. Eventually, she dies from radiation sickness.

"See," our grandmother tells us at the time, our mother's mother, who knew the Green family from way back.

"See what?" we ask. Claudia and I are, by then, in our teens. Our grandmother tells us this story:

"There once was a boy who had a pet fish, a trained carp. The boy had taught it to live out of water—at first, only for a few seconds; then a few minutes; then for hours at a time, and, finally, forever. The two of them went almost every place together. Until one day, when the boy was taking his bath, the carp fell into the tub and drowned."

"So?" we say, when she stops talking. Her stories, sometimes, have a point.

"So," she answers. "It goes to show; say no to where you come from long enough, you'll surely forget who you are. It can't help but lead to a bad end."

Our mother overhears our conversation. "Please," she says. "Why do you fill the children's heads with such nonsense?"

But all this comes later. The time I am speaking about is before. When I am eight, for instance. That year, Renee and her mother, briefly, come into my life. Renee's mother has a number tattooed on her arm, in blue, just below her elbow. The other mothers crowd around her and converse in whispers. Renee is older than I am, perhaps eleven. She is slender and long waisted, but with short legs and wide hips. She has long dark hair. She is the only one of us who knows how to dance. She and her mother dance together to phonograph records played in our living room. They know all the latest steps. The other mothers watch. They can hardly contain their enthusiasm. A year or so later, Renee and her mother move away. I know nothing else about them.

Age ten. I read all the books I can find on the subject. *World War II—the Jewish Question* is how they are listed in the nearest branch of our public library, the only one within walking distance. If *Holocaust* is a term in use then, no one I know uses it. The books are from the adult department. My mother lends me her card. The librarian isn't pleased, but abides by the rules. Attempting to appease her, I also take out fairy tales from the children's room, "Hansel and Gretel" for instance. I will be an adult before I am struck by its parallels and see that it is just another version of the Holocaust, with a happier ending, for children.

Except for the funny pages in the Sunday *Herald Tribune*, I do not read newspapers. When we have current events quizzes in school, sporadic and unannounced, I frequently fail them. Barry Goldfarb, a child in my class who distinguishes himself in no other way, at least in my memory, regularly gets one hundred. I discount the importance of quizzes. Tests are what count, I tell myself.

Not until I finish college do I begin to look at newspapers regularly, and then only for a few years, after which I avoid them, having persuaded myself that reading them is a waste of time; that they are, mainly, purveyors of bad news and gossip and forecasts, often contradictory, that can't be counted on. Nevertheless, there are two headlines that have stayed fixed in my mind from childhood: STALIN IS DEAD, and ROSENBERGS EXECUTED. I can close my eyes and see them even now. Each is set in very large, very thick, black as a funeral letters. I see this, too: a newspaper, held out in my mother's hands, a glimpse of a photograph, a dead man who, to the best of my memory, lies flat on his back on top of his casket, for viewing.

"I think it's a good thing for the Jews," my mother says. Breakfast is delayed while she peruses the article. Then, over scrambled eggs, sausage and toast, she and my father discuss it. "Good for which Jews?" I ask. "Is it good for us?" "Don't be silly," she tells me. "It's good for the Jews who are still in Russia." My father's family is from Russia. Does she mean it's good for them? Perhaps when some of them were coming here, some other ones got left behind? "Not so far as I know," my father says, though, when I raise the subject.

Surely there is a second photograph, but as hard as I try, I can't remember it with certainty. I think two people must have been in it, the Rosenbergs. The picture was taken, perhaps, at an earlier, happier time; or, possibly it was taken on the way to their execution. Were they briefly reunited, then, in that last hour, just before they died? I don't know. "It's bad for the Jews," my father says. "Which Jews?" "All of them." As far as I can tell, it isn't a question of guilty or not, or even of the execution itself. It is the name that concerns my father; Rosenberg, a Jewish name that calls attention to the rest. But does it call attention to us? Is our own last name, Ross, even Jewish? I ask Claudia, but she doesn't know either.

"Anyway," I say, "we're really Ethical Culturists."

"Jewish Ethical Culturists," she answers, and couldn't care less. Claudia still plans to be Catholic when she grows up, though now that we no longer live across the street from the Catholic school, I have changed my mind.

When I am twelve and Claudia is fourteen, we join the BBGs. We are B'nai, B'rith Girls. Our mother, surprisingly, encourages us in this direction. Perhaps, in relocating from Manhattan to Queens, she too has had a change of mind, or heart, when it comes to religion. Why Claudia joins, I have no idea. An oratory contest is sponsored that first year. No one in our chapter seems eager to be in it. Someone nominates me. I discuss it with my mother who offers to help me with my speech. She suggests, for my topic, anti-Semitism, and the concentration camps. She writes about Auschwitz, Dachau, Buchenwald; in language that seethes with her fury, she underscores that what happened in Europe must never be allowed to happen, anywhere, ever again. She helps me memorize this speech, and coaches me on saying it aloud. Even though I am the youngest girl in the contest, I win first prize at the state level. My mother is pleased. BBG pays my way to Chicago for the national competition in August. I travel there by train. This time I give not only my mother's speech, but an extemporaneous one as well that will count one-third toward my final score. I draw "Ecclesiastes" for my topic, and elaborate on the verse that states "to everything there is a season, and a time to every purpose under heaven." I concentrate on love and hate, and war and peace. First, second, and third place winners are announced. This time, I come in second. The judges shake our hands, and girls rush forward to congratulate us. After I have extricated myself from so many well-wishers, I telephone my mother with the news. She confirms my original opinion: "Second place is not the same as first."

By fall, both Claudia and I have quit the BBGs. By the time our mother notices, she, too, has lost interest. Finally, she has read B'nai B'rith's charter, including its membership policy. In order to join one must be "Jewish. . .and of good moral character." Our mother believes in democracy; she is opposed, without exception, to all exclusionary clauses and restrictive covenants.

She is opposed to other things, too; and though our father only rarely joins her discussion of these matters, it is clear he often shares her point of view. Neither one of them, for instance, will buy anything that's German made. In fact, they prefer to avoid all things that originate in Europe, and also Japan. Even our bicycles, which are not racers, are made in

America. Their disdain for what is German, however, goes far beyond just manufactured items. It is all encompassing. It isn't until I'm grown up, though, that I understand, fully, to what extent our lives were shaped by counteractive rules.

Here is an example. Germans followed orders without question; they believed in obedience. Claudia and I were taught to challenge every rule; even our mother's. "Make your bed!" "Straighten your room!" "Clean your plate!" "Why?" "Why?" "Why?" The last one was easy. Children were starving all over Europe. "If we eat our food, how will that help them?" We took turns posing this question. It was the only one for which our parents had no patience. "Don't be fresh," they told us. Claudia and I still clean our plates. Even in my anorexic stage, I ate what was in front of me, a lettuce leaf, three cheerios, a seedless grape; to this day, the only diet I can follow is forgoing mealtimes altogether.

Here is another. It is not true that every German citizen actively participated in the Holocaust. Some only stood by and watched. Some even disapproved, perhaps. It wasn't a lesson lost on our mother. Standing up and being counted was the least one had to do. Along with her, we wrote letters, signed and collected petitions, paraded with picket signs, and made donations to democratic causes. But all of our efforts were still not sufficient.

Therefore, counseled by our mother, Claudia and I stopped saying "liberty and justice for all," when we said the "Pledge of Allegiance" every morning in school. "When there is, the girls will say it," our mother explained to the principal. When "under God" was added to the Pledge, we didn't say that either. Our mother sent a note. "Separation of church and state is more than just a theory," she wrote.

Religion was also partly to blame for our mother's disapproval of the Girl Scouts, whose chapters met in churches or, sometimes, in synagogues. "Religion has no place in social clubs," she said. That was not the main reason, however, that Claudia and I didn't join. Scouts wore uniforms. So did the Germans. Being a soldier was one thing; being a child was another. It was a bad idea to mix the two, according to our mother.

During the Korean "conflict" certain safety measures were introduced into our school — air raid drills for instance. When the sirens sounded, we slumped to the floor and hid under our desks, actually large wooden tables at each of which sat four or six children. We were taught to place one hand over the backs of our necks, and to use our other one to shield our heads. "How stupid can they get?" my mother asked my father. "It sounds like a good idea to me," the other mothers said.

Sometimes, we children discussed it among ourselves, in the hallways or on the playground. "The reason you have to cover your head," Barry Goldfarb thoughtfully explained, "is to keep from getting a concussion in case a bomb makes the table fall down."

Dog tags were also distributed that year. These were small metal plates, each stamped with its new owner's name, age, and address. They were to be worn around our necks on beaded metal chains. Both tag and chain were noticeably sturdy, and evidently made to last. "Don't ever take these off," the teachers warned, as they called us, one by one, to the front of the room to get our tags. "Not even when we take a bath?" some child asked. "Never," said the teacher. "In case of war, the tag is your protection. All children will wear them."

"Not my child," our mother said, when Claudia and I got home from school and showed her ours. "Take that off this minute." We told our mother what the teachers said. "It only goes to show you can't believe everything you hear. The tags are for record keeping; purely so someone will know your name when you're dead," she answered. The next day she gave us a note to take to school. "Another note?" said Claudia. "It's getting boring." But even so, she gave it to the principal.

"Well, a tag, after all," I said, later, to Claudia. "This time, she's probably right." Claudia didn't care. She had bought herself a plain gold cross with money saved from her allowance. She wore it, day and night, on a chain around her neck, inside her clothes, hidden from our mother.

When I see, or hear about, "Safe Child" fingerprinting programs now, in schools, or shopping malls, sponsored by local police departments, I think of my mother. I hear her voice inside my head. "Some safe," she says, and means by it, let the police catch criminals and leave the children be.

She warned us often, as we were growing up, never to let ourselves be fingerprinted. In this, she was strongly supported by our father. If they gave reasons, and probably they did, I don't recall them. Claudia and I worried, though, about those prints we'd only left behind by accident. "Stop smudging," our mother used to say. "Why do the two of you have to rub up against everything all of the time?" We were erasing, eradicating evidence. Of what? Who knew! We did know this: A person didn't have to be guilty to be in trouble with the law. We'd been raised on cautionary tales our mother told us. It wasn't just the Rosenbergs, either. There were Sacco and Vanzetti, all nine of the Scottsboro boys and, saddest of all to our mother, J. Robert Oppenheimer, a man who believed in the same thing she did, a free America with civilians in charge.

It was hard, as we were growing up, remembering all the things to be against. It hasn't gotten easier. We are against all infringements on freedom: pre-employment drug or lie-detection testing, random stops and searches, warrantless seizures. "What about AIDS?" Vergil asks, and reminds me of the Chinese Communist man who said, "In America you will never wipe out venereal disease. Everybody has a right to have it." I relent, somewhat. "Perhaps public health testing for communicable diseases has its place," I reply. "But not for drugs?" he asks. "Not for drugs." "You're inconsistent," he tells me. "What worries me more than AIDS is the pilot who flies sky high on cocaine with me in his plane. What about him?" I have no easy answer, only the precepts from my childhood:

"Don't tell anyone anything. It isn't anybody's business. Tell the least that is required." Selecting the precise dividing line is always the problem. Just filling in a form can be hard.

This happened during the last census that was taken. A woman came to the door and left a questionnaire with me, to be filled in and returned. I filled it in. How many people reside in your residence? Two adults and one child, I entered in the place provided. All other spaces I left blank. I put the form in its envelope and mailed it back. A woman from the Census Bureau telephoned. "You left some spaces blank," she told me. "I need more information." "Yes?" I said. "What are you?" she asked. "What are we what?" "Black? White? Asian? Other?" "I have no idea," I said. "There is a penalty," she told me. "For what?" I asked. "For non-compliance. You are required by the Federal government to answer census questions. It's the law." "Is there a penalty for not knowing?" I asked. "No, there is no penalty for that." There was silence on the line. It seemed we'd reached an impasse. I yielded, a little. "You can send someone here, if you'd like, to look us over and decide."

When months had passed, and no one came, I thought I'd won. "Won what?" asked Zina, Vergil's daughter and mine. She was in high school at the time. I wasn't sure, but something. Then, at a conference, I met a librarian from the Census Bureau, and related my story. He told me what happens in such cases. "The Bureau assigns coded numbers designating choice of race. It depends on where you live, and other factors." "Oh," I said, disappointed. I imagined us being divided this way: one black, one white, one other. I saw, then, I hadn't won at all.

I told my mother. She didn't understand my problem. "I think you spend too much time worrying about the wrong things and not enough time on what's important," she said. "Like what?" I asked. It wouldn't be the first time I'd gotten things wrong. "Health care, for instance," she told me. She was, at that time, in the midst of a campaign seeking passage of a national health plan. She sent me a list of names of politicians to write to, and I did.

Afterward, I discussed the matter with Claudia. She remembered things exactly my way. "It's hard keeping up, though," she said. "And it doesn't get easier." She told me about her car. "I insisted on buying an American one, even though it cost more. Everybody told me I was crazy. And you know, they were right! All the parts, I found out later, were made in other countries. I tell you, Mirra, other people live by less complicated rules. I've been trying to give up some of hers. You'd be surprised how hard it is." It sounded funny to me when she said it, but later, when I recalled her words under different circumstances, they resounded with sorrow.

These were the circumstances. We had taken my father to the hospital. He was truly on his last legs by then. At my mother's request, I'd called for an ambulance. She and I followed it, in her car, to the Emergency Room. There my father sat in a hospital wheelchair. We stood one on each side of him. The admitting clerk asked him the usual questions. By this stage, his voice was so low as to be barely audible, and usually my mother was the only one who could make out what he said. Therefore, in all transactions, she served as his interpreter, and sometimes answered for him.

"Religious persuasion?" was the clerk's last question. My parents looked at each other in silence. I looked at both of them. The admitting clerk watched us all. Finally, she asked, "Does he have some religion? Is he Catholic? Jewish? Protestant?" "Oh," my mother said, though not right away. "Yes, he does." She paused before going on. Then she said, "Jewish. He's Jewish." My father confirmed this by nodding.

Afterward, as she and I were leaving, my mother said to me, "Religious persuasion, after all. Who knew what she meant? Besides," she added, when we were in the car, "I don't really see, anyway, what business it is of hers."

"Well," I said, shrugging. "It's just something they put on the form."

A few days later my mother rented a hospital bed and hired around-the-clock nursing aides. Then she called for an ambulance, and brought my father home, for the last time.

The Galloper

When Louise told her husband Harold that she had quit
her job as Publications Director for a prestigious international
chemicals concern to take a new one as an exerciser at the
racetrack, all he could think to ask was, "Yes, but what will
you do with all of your clothes?" Louise had wondered that
herself. Well, what did she do with them now? It was true
they filled her closets, spilling over into the children's,
David's and Dede's who were away in college, sometimes
even turning up in Harold's. She didn't really understand it.
Louise didn't care *that* much for clothes, and seldom wore the
ones she owned. Most often when she needed something to
be warm or go to work in, she went into Dede's room and
hunted in her closet, found something old and put it on.
Sometimes what she put on turned out to be hers, handed
down to Dede unworn years ago. Louise's own clothes, for
the most part, hung new on the hangers they'd come on,
faintly scented with the moth flakes and lavender she used to
preserve them.

Occasionally, when she considered them, Louise recalled
with discomfort a story her mother used to tell her about a
woman named Basia Gittel who was obsessed by clothes.
Louise had forgotten most of the story, except for its ending
which warned that if a person hung more clothes in her closet
than she could reasonably wear, devils would come by night

to dance in them and haunt their owner's dreams. Louise sometimes wondered if she, like Basia Gittel, was obsessed by clothes. But in the end, she always decided no, carefully explaining to herself that she only bought so many because it gave her something to do, and also it took her mind off of work. The last part of the warning, however, Louise believed was true. Her own dreams had pursued her through the years, though hardly ever any more since she'd started her new job. Now she slept more and dreamed less. Well, she told herself, it was only natural. Working at a racetrack was nothing like directing publications from a desk.

There were the horses, for one thing. Louise could not recall a time when she hadn't loved horses. There was not a single thing about them that displeased her. Even the scent of horses in the air filled her with excitement, like a physical wave that overrode her and hurried her in their direction. When she was ten, she had insisted on riding lessons with such vehemence and frequency that her parents, used to a mild-mannered child, had given in and said yes. Louise's mother had told Louise's father in the end, "People of substance ride horses; maybe she'll meet some." She hadn't envisioned her oldest daughter working at a racetrack, though, knee-deep in manure, shoveling, the way she imagined her now. Nor was it far from the truth.

"I'm a writer," Louise told Mr. D., the trainer, the day she telephoned for an appointment. "I'd like to interview you." She meant, I'd like to work for you. "I'll do anything," she informed him once she was there. "Besides, animals take to me," she said.

Mr. D. believed her. Unseen, he had watched as Louise climbed from her car and looked around outside his barn. He saw her read the sign, "Beware of Dog." Then he waited as Thor approached her. Thor was a large black mastiff, although to Louise that day he looked like a cross between a Labrador Retriever and a St. Bernard. He had a carrot in his mouth.

Louise, who had never seen a dog before with a carrot in its mouth, also had no idea what steps one could take to beware. Therefore, she held out her hand and hoped for the best. Thor wagged his tail and gave Louise the carrot. Mr. D. stepped out of the barn. "You must be Louise," he said.

Afterward, whenever she remembered, Louise brought carrots with her to the track. Thor always seemed pleased. Not that he needed Louise's; he had a fine supply of his own, furnished by James, Mr. D.'s son.

James was a trainer in training and also his father's business manager. "Why else did I spend so much money sending him to college?" his father liked to ask. It was true James had graduated from a small, expensive, well-regarded business college in Maine. But concerning the reason for his going, his father mostly was joking. Mr. D. believed in education. He was not alone in this. Louise was surprised to discover how many of those employed at the track were college graduates. Even among those whose work included mucking out stalls, there were quite a few degrees. Well, why should it have surprised Louise? Hers was one of them, although, naturally, a degree in English literature, such as she had, was not necessarily the best kind for the job. Gillian, a female jockey, had majored in equestrian studies in Maryland.

"Well, sure," Harold said when Louise told him. "Maryland, I'm not surprised. It probably ran in her family." But it hadn't. Gillian's mother, as Louise enjoyed informing Harold, was a grade school teacher, and Gillian's father owned a hardware store. "I see," Harold said, then added, "I don't suppose this Gillian has children, or is even married?"

"Are you?" Louise asked the next time they spoke. Gillian was not, but other female jockeys were, she pointed out, or had been. Louise, who normally avoided asking personal questions, persisted: "If you ever do get married, and have children, could you keep on riding?" Gillian shrugged, the topic clearly of no interest to her.

"I'm never going to," she said.

It occurred to Louise for the first time that minute that this had never occurred to her before—a person had that choice.

Later, when she spoke with her mother on the telephone, and tried to explain to her about Gillian, she realized it was the certainty and not the choice that so amazed her. "The thing is, how can a person be so certain about what she wants to do with her life? How can she *know*?" Louise asked her mother. Louise was seldom certain about anything. Well, she was against hunting and people who did it, but otherwise her capacity to be surprised when other people knew the things they knew seemed limitless. She was especially surprised since she, Louise, was supposed to be exceptionally intelligent. At least, she had always been considered so in school. Well, Louise did know that school was nothing like life. In fact, she sometimes thought that school was the last and only place where being smart and getting ahead were one and the same, or almost the same. Louise had never liked school any better than she liked work, but then Louise had never quite grasped the point about getting ahead. Ahead to where? She recalled a novel she'd read once in which a recovering escapee from a mental institution had watched the other people in the book going back and forth to their jobs, earning their livings. Yes, the woman had wondered; then after they earned them, how did they live? Louise frequently wondered that herself.

But now she only sighed, as she heard her mother say, "You knew enough to quit your job." Louise felt relieved when their conversation came to an end. She knew there was no way adequately to explain to her mother that quitting her job had not involved any choice. That was exactly the point. She'd done the only thing she could. She'd no longer been able to breathe at work.

Well, she'd been having trouble breathing, period, but the worst times had been in her office, and they'd gotten increasingly worse as each day progressed. She started out every morning by taking deep breaths, then deeper ones. By midafternoon, she'd be gasping for air. Finally, she remembered having felt that same way in school. Then, she'd been allowed to stay home. Her mother kept her in bed and gave her allergy medicine. Louise listened to the radio. It was much better than being in class, although she would have been hard pressed to say why. She hated making dioramas, or milk carton drawbridges for science; she couldn't draw a subway map or a family tree, or see why anyone would want to. Nor could she stand having to do social studies research as part of a committee. She wheezed instead.

Maybe it's some sort of allergy that's causing my current problem, Louise had thought, as she sat in her office one day, recalling her childhood and trying to breathe. It was then she had taken herself to a doctor.

"Perhaps I have asthma?" she suggested helpfully.

"No," the doctor said as he listened with his stethoscope against her chest. "Your lungs could not be clearer."

"Then why can't I breathe?" Louise asked.

"You're breathing fine," he said. Well, sure, in his office she was, but she couldn't stay there forever. She had to earn a living after all.

At home that night she came across a book that Harold had been given at work. *Home Health Maintenance* was its title. It had been issued free by the same company that insured the workers' health and hoped to keep them in it. Under *breathing problems* was a section on HYPERVENTILATION. Louise read it carefully. The symptoms described seemed very much like hers. According to the book, they could usually be alleviated by having the patient breathe into and out of a paper bag. Louise tried it. It worked. She wasn't surprised, but she didn't see how it could help her. She couldn't sit at her desk all day with a paper bag covering her face. How would she explain it? She couldn't very well say, I cannot breathe at work because I cannot bear my job. Enthusiasm was considered an important component of effectiveness in a position such as hers. No one in the company would care to know that the point of what she did eluded her. She resigned instead.

It was only minutes after Louise's conversation with her mother that Louise called her sister in Mamaroneck. Ellen was the only one she knew who usually saw eye to eye with her, and had envied Louise her new position. Ellen was home that week, recuperating from minor surgery, the removal of a small growth on her back that had been there for years. "I don't mind telling you, it makes me nervous," she told Louise. Ellen meant it made her nervous staying home from work, and not about the growth, which she had always known was nothing. Ellen worked as a secretary and general office manager for a group of obstetricians. She felt it was a great improvement over what she used to do. She had formerly been a teacher. "Teaching is a good profession for a woman," their mother told them frequently as they were growing up. "You have your summers off, and spring and winter recess." Ellen sometimes thought their mother should have mentioned what it would be like between-times. "The thing is," Ellen pointed out now to Louise, sounding worried, "if you stay home too long, they find someone else to catch up on your work, someone more efficient, and pleasanter to have around. Anyone," she said, a note of despair in her voice, "would be pleasanter to have around and more efficient."

By the time Louise hung up the telephone, she was beaming. Well, why wouldn't she be? Anyone could see her job was so much better than her sister's. It was better than anyone's. The only thing that might be even better, she thought, would be to live right there at the track, close to the horses and all the time. Naturally, this wasn't the first time she'd thought this. She had thought of it even before going for her interview. "I could live here if it mattered," she had planned to say that day, then hadn't when she saw that no one cared. Now, suddenly, it mattered to Louise.

She weighed her situation carefully. At home she was often alone, Harold being frequently away on business trips. Her room at the track would be free. She wouldn't need to commute. Nor would she need a telephone. There was a pay phone in the hall, although no one she knew had its number. It was a consideration that appealed to Louise. She liked making calls, but the sound of a telephone ringing was almost more than she could bear, and even when one wasn't ringing, she knew that it could start to any moment and if she picked it up, she might find out exactly what she did not want to know.

Ever since Louise's father had died several years ago with no warning, struck down by a van, Louise understood that life was lived every day on the brink of disaster. She tried to stay on her guard. Whenever she began to feel the least bit happy, or safe, she reminded herself it could just be that she hadn't found out yet. "Found out *what* yet, for goodness' sake?" Harold asked her in increasing exasperation. But Louise only shrugged. Anything, she'd think. Planes crashed, trains derailed; when Harold or the children traveled, Louise didn't want to know it. She tried not to think about cancer, and avoided articles on nuclear disaster. When Harold was in California, she pretended there was no such thing as an earthquake. Harold was in California now. Louise picked up the telephone and called her sister back.

"I've made up my mind," she announced. "I'm moving to the track." Ellen thought it was a wonderful idea.

"You're doing what?" Harold asked in disbelief when he got back from San Francisco. "You want to live in a barn when you have a carpeted room with a very nice view, a king-size bed, and walk-in closets the size of some people's houses?"

"Not a barn," she explained. "It's a dormitory. It's next to the barn. It would save me several hours of commuting every week."

"I see," Harold said. He wondered what she planned to do with the hours saved. She hadn't been clothes-shopping in months.

"It's not as if you're home every night. There's hardly ever anybody here but me. I'll come back on school vacations, and on weekends when you're home."

"The cat's here," he said. "What will you do with the cat?"

The cat, Louise saw right away, could go with her. "A race-track," she pointed out, "is a good place for a cat." It was the truth. People were forever dropping off their cats and litters of kittens, hoping that people who looked after horses would look out for other animals, too, which they did. Not just cats, either, and dogs, but chickens and goats, which they said made good pets for the horses. Louise believed, though, they did it from kindness. It confirmed a long-held view of hers that people who lived with horses, and didn't worry about hair on their clothes or mud on their shoes, would have to be a step up from the rest of the world. It was one more reason she wanted to move.

Moving itself was no problem. Finally, her children had turned out to be of some use. They'd taught her through the years how to pack. She'd learned by watching them, and crit-icizing. She saw now she'd been wrong. A person didn't need a suitcase. As she had seen them do so many times, Louise made little trips back and forth between closet and car, filling its trunk with what she needed. Well, she didn't need much: dungarees, shirts, sweaters, and boots. She saw with satisfac-tion her closets already had begun to empty. She liked to think they had emptied on their own. She wanted to believe the clothes had taken off by themselves, and pictured them at late-night parties, demented soirées, danced in by demons as in her mother's story, parts of which had started drifting back to her. But the truth was that since she had stopped buying clothes, she had also stopped sprinkling the ones that she owned with moth flakes and lavender, and now that they no longer were scented, however faintly, Dede had begun appro-priating them. She had taken most of them to college.

The last thing that Louise put in her car was her favorite blanket. It was a quilted affair, lined with wool batting and covered in silk, an extravagance, she knew. But still, Louise believed that if possession of a blanket could keep away the cold, it would be foolish to deny herself its comfort. Naturally, she did not mean the cold of winter only; she also meant the cold that clutched at one's heart when one considered unbefallen dangers still to be confronted, a telephone that rang at night, for instance. Louise looked around. There was nothing left to do. She picked up the cat, climbed into the car, and drove to the track.

In almost no time, Louise knew she had made the right move. Life lived at the track was nothing like commuting. Of course, it was also true Louise had been promoted. She no longer did hot-walking, nor was she a groom. She was a galloper exclusively. She spent her mornings on the track exercising horses. Afterward, she soaked in long, hot baths and rubbed herself down with Beagle Oil. Then she sat with her cat in her lap and read books. Sometimes she played tug-of-war with Thor and his carrot. She regarded Thor thoughtfully at times like those and reflected. It was true he was only a dog, and yet he had found what he wanted and stuck to it. A person could do worse; most of them did. That was why when James urged her now and then to ride for his father, Louise resisted.

"It's all in the hands," he told her. "You've got a winner's touch. A jockey can get rich," he said. "You could be famous."

Louise believed him, and was sometimes tempted. But then she'd look again at Thor, find a carrot for him, and remind herself, she wasn't in it for the money.

Dr. Akiri

Not when I first notice it, because when I first notice it, I'm certain it's nothing, but two or three months afterward, when it still is where it was, at the bottom left corner of my left breast, that is the time I run through my mind quickly the seven warning signs of cancer a person needs to know. Or is it five? A lump that changes, any sort of mole. Or could it be a mole that changes, and any sort of lump? It occurs to me that anyway I no longer see the seven signs enumerated everywhere I look. I think perhaps the rules have changed; maybe there are more signs now, too numerous for just one list. I telephone my doctor's office.

Up until the morning of the day of my appointment, I am fairly unconcerned. Lumps in my family come and go, a familial trait like size ten feet. It is only that this one has stayed so long that I am even a little apprehensive.

"How long have I had this here?" I ask my husband. "Two months? Do you think two months?"

"Oh," he answers in his offhand way, "perhaps a year, nine months anyway."

Can he be thinking of a pregnancy? "Nine months," I yell at him. "A year," I shout. "Do you mean to say that you have let me walk around this way that long? What kind of a hus-

91

band are you anyway?" After this he won't discuss it with me any more. I can't say I really blame him.

"Call and tell me what the doctor says," he says, kissing me good-bye. "I'm sure it isn't anything," he adds, going through the door. He is leaving on a business trip. He has his suitbag over one arm. "I'll be in Philadelphia tonight," he says, "in Harrisburg tomorrow." He is a businessman. He takes a lot of business trips.

"I'm sure it isn't anything," I tell my doctor, wondering why I'm even here. "It's only that I've had it for some time, two months, I think. Maybe even for a year."

"Ummhumm," he says, and nods. "Probably it isn't anything. Still," he adds, surprising me, "it wouldn't hurt to have a mammogram."

It seems the possibility exists, bearing further study, that a mammogram can cause as well as diagnose some cancers. Didn't I read that somewhere once?

"Life's like that," the doctor tells me when I put it to him. "You have to weigh one chance against another; in the end it's up to you." It's this philosophy of his that makes me trust him as a doctor. Doctors are a dime a dozen who act like they are God. "Well," he says, noting my reluctance, "if you'd rather, we can watch it for a while." Watch it do what, I wonder.

That evening, I telephone my sister. Her husband is a sort of doctor.

"A doctor," she yells at me anytime that I misuse the word, "is a person with a doctoral degree. A physician is someone whom you see when you are sick."

These days I nearly always get it right, or else correct myself immediately. "Why don't you make an appointment with the doctor, I mean physician," I'm always saying whenever someone tells me something's wrong and asks for my opinion. Lisbeth's husband is a doctor. He does medical research, but he's not a physician. "It's almost just as good," our mother has been overheard to say, though not to us. Still I assume he has many physicians among his acquaintances. It turns out I won't need them. Lisbeth has connections.

"Probably it's nothing," she tells me cheerfully. "I know someone you can see. The same thing happened to me last year. I also didn't want to have a mammogram." She is surprised I don't remember. This sister, who left her job at Bloomingdale's, done in by the new computerized cash registers whose operation she could never master ("I can't even get the damned things to open," she'd said), now works for a neurologist. Occasionally she assists him doing spinal taps.

"Spinal taps?" our mother says to me on the telephone from Florida. "Lisbeth is doing spinal taps?"

Sometimes, rarely, I will call Lisbeth at her work. She always sounds distracted.

"Wait a minute," she says, "I have to write this down. Hold on," she tells me, "I don't want to get the samples mixed. . ."

"I can call you another time," I say.

"Oh no," she answers. "It's all right. It's just such a nuisance having to get a patient to come back. . ." Her voice trails off. I see blood and spinal fluid. When she returns, her conversation is of something else entirely. I much prefer speaking with her when she's home.

"The doctor's name," she says, at home now, "is a bit unusual. Have you got a pencil?" She spells it for me. "A K I R I. Akiri," she says. "Dr. Akiri. I think he's Indian."

"Indian," I repeat, with a sinking feeling. I have known Indians in my life, and never understood a single one of them. Well, I haven't known *that* many Indians, but surely much more than average. I worked for a government agency in the sixties whose business was with "underdeveloped" countries. I believe we don't say underdeveloped anymore, but I recall what it was like.

"Pardon me," I'd say. "Can you repeat that. I'm sorry. I didn't understand."

Indians do not like it when an American who does not even speak English properly acts as if she cannot understand them. "English, we speak the Queen's English," all the Indians I've ever known have told me in annoyance. "Over here you only speak American."

"Yes," I'd apologize. "I know." In the sixties I apologized for anything. Sometimes I still do.

"Indian accents are so hard to understand," I say to my sister.

"Oh, I wouldn't worry too much about that," she tells me. "I understood him all right. Besides," she adds, "he doesn't say that much."

"How much is it?" I ask.

"How much what?" she repeats a bit blankly.

"How much money should I bring?"

"Oh," she says, "I don't remember. It seems to me he wasn't that expensive."

I consider whom I'm asking. Among Lisbeth's many duties is to inform prospective patients on her office telephone: "The first visit is $500. Please bring full payment when you come. I'm sorry, but we don't accept personal checks." When she has to complete insurance forms, the patient still must pay the full amount, then pay ten dollars more on account of Lisbeth's time. "It's really an outrage," she has said to me, outraged, then added, "Well, I don't make the policy. It's only a job."

"What does he do?" I ask. "I mean what does he do for what I will pay him?" I try to imagine the visit. How long can it take to examine a breast? I recall the old joke I never thought funny: Does your mother know what you do for a living?

"I don't really remember," she says. "It was a while ago. I remember he looked at my neck."

Reluctantly, I ask her what I really want to know. "Will he do a pap test?" I inquire suspiciously, calculating how many hours it will be between my morning shower and his office, wanting to make a good impression on the doctor.

"Of course not. He's a breast surgeon," she tells me. I am relieved.

In his office I am relieved again. I sit in front of him, he asks me questions. Japanese, I think, he's Japanese. I am so glad to know that. How could my sister have thought Indian. Indian and Japanese do not even look alike. Had he been Indian, I would have had to sit here smiling, idiotically, pretending that I understood whatever he was saying. Japanese I can understand just fine. Besides, I consider Hiroshima. If anyone would know about cancer, wouldn't it be a Japanese?

"Did you come alone?" the doctor asks.

Why is he asking? Does he think that I'm brave? Or does he need to know whom to tell if it turns out I have cancer?

My husband would have come with me, except he's on a business trip, this time Seattle. I keep this information to myself. I realize the doctor might not be too interested in knowing. My husband probably would have changed his plans had I insisted, but somehow having to insist seemed to me to miss the point. "I'm sure it's nothing," he had said just as he was leaving.

I want my mother, I had thought then. Actually, not my mother. I wanted *a* mother, someone who would make a fuss. My mother never makes a fuss. She would have done me no good whatsoever.

"Dr. Akiri's rather distant," my sister had warned me. I seem to have an affinity for distant doctors. Maybe just for distant men. If Dr. Akiri were to run for president, no doubt I'd vote for him. I wonder if he's married.

"Has anyone in your family had cancer?" he asks. I knew he would ask that. I have already practiced my answer while riding the train.

"Yes," I say. "My father's mother and his sister. Also my cousin, the sister's daughter." He nods and writes this down. I wonder if cancer runs in my family.

I follow the nurse into the examination room and take off my jacket and brand new silk blouse. She hangs my only lace bra on the door. "Oh," she says, "it's so little. Isn't that cute." For just a moment I can't believe I have actually heard her say that. Usually I would be offended, but this time I am not. Japanese are small. Probably the doctor will think I am exactly the right size. Perhaps, thinking that, he won't find cancer. It is true. He doesn't.

"I am certain not," he tells me. "Absolute, positive." I believe him. He exudes confidence, integrity and good will. "Still," he says, "it must come out." I am surprised to hear him say this. "It should be examined by a pathologist," he informs me, "for the one chance in 10,000 I am wrong. Even so, I say to you, don't worry. I am not ever wrong. Besides, if it stays, it just gets bigger." He says if I have time to wait, he can remove it in the office. I have time. Afterward he shows it to me. "It does not look even a little bit like cancer," he assures me. When the pathologist report comes back, it will turn out he is right. It isn't cancer.

Leaving his office, I pay brief attention to the people waiting in the waiting room. They seem to know one another slightly. I think it is likely as much as one can bear to know another cancer patient. "Good luck," they keep on saying. "Good luck," when someone new comes in. "Good luck," when someone's name is called to see the doctor. "Good luck," when someone pays her bill and leaves. They come in pairs, but the patients all are women. Do women get more cancer? Do men come on another day? Is it some ancient honored Eastern custom? Only then do I remember—a doctor who specializes in breasts, after all. "Seven years," a man says joyfully, pointing toward his wife. "We're among the lucky ones." I look at him and think he could go home tonight and die—massive heart attack. What is it about cancer then— except for its cure?

That evening, I call my sister to thank her for telling me about Dr. Akiri.
"Japanese," I tell her. "He is Japanese."
"Japanese," she says wonderingly. "Are you sure Japanese? I always thought Indian. Maybe Pakistani. How do you know Japanese?"
"He told me that he was."
"Told you," she repeats. She has always had this habit.

Some people probably don't notice it. But to me, it is like hearing my own echo. Like stereo, my husband has said more than once, amused, when you and she sit in the same room speaking.

"How did he happen to tell you?" my sister persists.

"He was talking on the telephone," I say. "To Sicily. After he hung up he told me that sometimes he talks also to Japan. Not to Japan, to family in Japan. 'I still have family there,' he said. 'I go back once a year.'"

"Oh," says Lisbeth faintly, forced at last to see that she was wrong and I am right. I do not need to add for emphasis, thank goodness, that over my left breast, as he was cutting, he and the nurse were holding a conversation about air-conditioners.

"Japanese," she'd said, "don't make air-conditioners. Funny, isn't it? They make everything else."

"Don't be silly," the doctor told her, pulling at my adenoma. That is what he called it—not cyst, worse than cyst, better than tumor—adenoma. "Of course Japanese make air-conditioners. Japanese make everything. Only you don't let us send them here." His use of *us* and *you* took me by surprise. Again, I thought of Hiroshima. Surely he wouldn't hold it against me. I was hardly born then. Besides, I'm anti-nuclear. I would not even go so far as to have a mammogram. Even my husband, who is occasionally in energy, will deal only with fusion. Fusion is not the same as fission. I considered telling this to the doctor, but it seemed too complicated to explain. Besides, by then, he was already up to stitches. (In a week, when I return to my regular doctor to have the stitches taken out, he and his nurse will be discussing the kind of screws she needs to buy to fix his gooseneck lamp. I wonder if such conversation is what they teach in medical school: Discuss a neutral topic to get the patient to relax.)

Enough is enough, I think. It has been a long day. I tell Lisbeth good-bye and hang up the phone. I fall asleep and dream that I have left my husband, the husband who is out of town on business in Seattle, for Dr. Akiri. I am now Mrs. Dr. Akiri.

In my dream I see my doctor husband pick up the telephone and shout into it, just as he did when I was sitting in his office. "Japan," he says when he hangs up. "You can hear the same as if the other person were sitting in this room." Why do people always say that, I wonder—just the same as in this room, and then still shout into telephone receivers. I love to listen when other people are talking on the telephone. "It's rude," my husband always says, the one away on business. "If a phone call is for someone else, then you should leave the room."

Dr. Akiri, I think, would not care if I stayed and listened. He wouldn't care if the whole world heard him. "Sicily," he had told me in his office hanging up the phone. "Tokyo," he'd said with pleasure, putting the receiver on the hook.

Now, in my dream, he says again, "You know, you can hear just the same as if the other person were sitting in this room. You know why?" It's the same question he'd raised in his office. I shake my head, as I did then, so he will tell me. He says, "I used to think on account of satellite. You know satellite? But not so." He smiles at me. "There is cable underneath the whole Pacific Ocean, California to Japan. Imagine," he says, imagining. I am surprised, both times, to see how he is so surprised by a scientific feat. I mean, he is after all a scientist himself. "Yes, science," he says. "But imagine cable going all the way from here to there."

My businessman husband is an engineer. Several weeks later, while he is briefly home, packing for another trip, I remember to ask him. "Is it really true about the cable?" He tells me yes. He is not at all surprised.

"Cable, satellite—they use them both," he says. "There's cable under the Atlantic Ocean," he points out to me. "It's been there for years—to Iceland, to England." Later I wonder if there is cable all the way to China, to Africa. How do they decide where to put it, where not to put it?

My doctor husband would say, "I don't know. Amazing, isn't it! I wonder how they know." My businessman husband only shrugs. It's all the same to him. "Nowadays you can dial direct to almost anywhere," he says. "It's just a matter of technology."

Sometime later I discuss my dream with my sister.

"Well, I think I wouldn't really like being married that much to a doctor, I mean a physician. I mean not to that kind of physician." I don't like to say oncologist, as though maybe only saying it could bring bad luck. "How would I feel knowing every night that he could be bringing cancer home to me on his hands?"

"It's not contagious," she tells me.

"We don't think it's contagious," I say. "But we don't really know, do we? What if it is? We don't know everything about cancer yet."

"Anything," she says. "We don't know anything about it really. Still," she goes on, "being married to an oncologist, if you got it, who'd have better care?" I think, but can't be sure, that she is joking.

"Ummm," I say, but actually I'm considering what it would be like going with my doctor husband every summer to Japan to visit family.

"How would it look if I were to take you with me on a company trip?" my businessman husband asked last month on his way to Tokyo. "How would it look taking you to Russia?" He is going to Russia sometime soon, certainly this year.

"How would it look for you to see St. Petersburg without me?" I ask him. "My father, for Pete's sake, was born in St. Petersburg." I hadn't meant to pun. My husband overlooks it, or maybe didn't notice. "You should have heard my mother when it was only Tokyo. Besides," I remind him, "you left me alone that time when I could have had cancer."

"Yes," he says. "But you didn't."

"I know," I persist, "but you didn't *know* that. I think you'd better take me with you when you go to Russia."

He doesn't say yes or no right away. But a week or so before he's scheduled to leave he tells me, "Pack your bag. Be sure your passport's current." My passport's always current.

While I'm packing, I say to him, "You know, for years whenever I have bought a bra I've thought, what if I get cancer? Supposing they remove a breast, all that money gone for nothing."

My husband looks at me in disbelief. "How about shoes," he asks, "or gloves? Why buy anything? Next year you could be dead." It happens I have thought of that, but I let the subject drop. I think he'd just as soon not know.

"I was worried about you," he tells me when we finally are in Russia. He is referring to my operation, looking at my breasts as I am getting dressed.

"Worried?" I ask. "Why? You said you knew all along that it was nothing."

"Well," he says, "I didn't want to worry you. There was no point in both of us being worried."

I think about Philadelphia, recall Seattle, but even so I'd rather not entirely disbelieve him. And after all, I am in Russia.

When we get home, I telephone my parents.

"You could have called from St. Petersburg," my husband says.

"St. Petersburg was lovely," I tell them from New York. "There was so much to see in Russia."

"Russia," my father says. "I have never understood why anyone would want to go to Russia. When we were living there, all we ever wanted was to leave."

"I'm not surprised," my husband says, when I tell him. It is one of the rare times I can remember that he and my father have seen eye to eye on anything.

That night I dream that I'm a Russian doctor. My husband, who's a radiologist, and I are attending a medical conference in Japan.

During my next conversation with my sister, I mention my dream. She says, "It's fairly common to dream you're married to a doctor."

"Do you dream that too?" I ask her, interested.

"Who, me? Why would I?" She sounds annoyed. "I am married to a doctor."

"That's right," I say. "Of course."

American Pastorale

Robert watched Susan pack. "Take farm clothes," he said, "and don't forget to feed the cat." Farm clothes were easy. Susan, an illustrator, worked in them. Dungarees and T-shirts were the mainstay of her wardrobe. Born and raised in the heart of Manhattan, she nevertheless considered herself a country person at heart. "I should have been born on a farm," she frequently said. Robert, literally born and raised on a farm, believed his wife had no idea what that life was like. It was mainly to give her some idea that he had planned this weekend trip to his uncle Ben's farm in Georgia.

Susan knew something of Georgia. As a bride years ago, she had passed through it with Robert. She recalled signs at the border, the one that said "Georgia Welcomes You" and ten feet beyond it another that read "The Klan Welcomes You." Neither she nor Robert had believed either sign. Robert is black, Susan is not. His color is not something she thinks about with any regularity, but sometimes, early in the morning, turning over in bed, for instance, she will notice. Or watching him step from the shower. "It's so cute," she told him once, "how you are brown all over."

Now, having finished packing, Susan carefully set out food and water for her cat. Actually, it had been the children's cat since they were small. With both of them now grown and off at college, Susan sometimes worried that the cat missed their attention. Robert thought the cat probably enjoyed weekends with everyone gone and the house to itself. "When we're here," their son Robbie explained, the last time he was, "we disrupt her routine." Susan watched speculatively as the cat, predictably turning what was meant for several meals into a single feast, began to eat.

Susan and Robert flew to Atlanta, stayed overnight at a hotel, and rented a car to drive to the farm. Susan was glad to see there were no signs. She understood it was a new South now.

They'd originally planned to start the drive in the morning, but Robert had some business to attend to. It was late afternoon by the time they got on the road, so it was already dark when they got lost; for miles there was nowhere to stop and no one to ask for directions. Susan hadn't realized nighttime was so dark in the country. She remembered a story her husband had told her once about when he was a child. He'd been with his mother on a bus in the country at night. They'd sat down in the first row of the black section. He was young enough that he didn't go to school yet, and his feet didn't reach the floor. One of them must have been swinging. It swung enough to kick the white seat in front of him. The driver stopped the bus and put Robert and his mother out, in the dark, in the country, miles from anyplace.

"What did you do?" Susan had asked.

"We walked miles to get home," Robert replied.

She preferred another story that he told: His mother and the children were at a county fair one night. Their car was pulled up to the fence along with all the others. A white man climbed onto its hood to get a better view. After a while he decided it would be fun to jump up and down.

"Probably he'd been drinking," Robert had said, relating the incident. "'If I were you I wouldn't do that anymore,' Mother told him. But the man didn't stop. Mother got her shotgun from the back of the car and pointed it at him."

"What happened then?" Susan had wanted to know.

"The man stopped jumping on the car, climbed down, and went away," said Robert.

Susan's thoughts were interrupted by Robert asking her if she was paying attention to the signs. "It's too dark to see them," she replied, then noticed they seemed to be entering what could pass for a town. They drove by an auto repair shop. Black men stood where the junked cars were, apparently joking, sounds of their laughter floating in the air. A few blocks farther was a gas station. The only people visible were white. At both places Robert tightened his grip on the steering wheel and kept going. Susan wondered uneasily if he was thinking of the rifle that he used to keep beneath the passenger seat for driving in the South. She'd always understood dangers that lurked at night in the city. Now she reflected, big as this country was, wherever one went in it, it seemed to be taking one's life in one's hands just to go out after dark. It was the ever-present sense of violence, she thought; whether anything actually developed or not seemed almost beside the point. About that time they found a telephone booth. Robert called for better directions, and after a few mis-starts, they finally arrived at his uncle's.

Susan found herself in the living room of a large suburban house, wondering where the farm was. She was introduced to Robert's relatives, hugged and kissed by his aunt Reesa, uncle Ben, and numerous cousins, only a few of whom still lived at home. "You could have asked anyone for directions," one of them said. "Everyone for miles knows Daddy."

Susan stepped back and looked around. Maybe, she started to decide, they'd sold the farm and moved to the suburbs. But right away she saw that was unlikely. The house was ancient. Its walls were covered almost completely by photographs, certificates, school papers, crayon drawings; knickknacks were everywhere. The family that lived here, Susan could see, had moved in long ago. If only Robert would communicate like a normal person, she told herself, she'd know what was what.

Robert watched Susan, bemused as usual at how well she

fit. Some weeks before they'd gone to see *Zelig*, the Woody Allen movie about a chameleon-like man. Susan, usually a Woody Allen fan, had found it tedious and pointless, but it had strongly reminded Robert of his wife. This minute, watching her, he thought again of the film. She had already started to look like his relations. Like them, she was small and delicately-featured. She had the same dark, thick hair, worn braided and knotted into intricate patterns. Even Susan's olive skin was hardly lighter than the lightest of his cousins. Robert remembered as a child thinking his aunt Reesa looked ghostly. She had been exceedingly thin. Now he wondered if maybe he had thought ghostly because she was so pale. Creole, he'd heard her called then.

It was almost midnight when Uncle Ben showed them to the room where they were to sleep. It was the first bedroom, facing the street. The bed in it had once belonged to Robert's great-grandmother, and had been carted from Alabama to Georgia by Uncle Ben when he'd moved. He pointed out to them a hole in the front window of the room, a bullet hole put there the previous winter by his middle daughter, Denise. "Freeze," Uncle Ben said she had warned the would-be intruder. When he hadn't, she'd fired, a bit wildly, and missed. "Well," Uncle Ben said, sounding pleased, "I gave her the gun loaded and cocked. It was the last time anybody tried to get in." Susan wondered, but didn't ask, what would have happened if one of the children, Denise's own baby for instance, had gotten hold of the gun first. Robert already thought she asked too many questions. A person could learn a lot, he regularly told her, just by waiting. Now, Susan waited patiently as Uncle Ben told them goodnight. "We'll drive to the farm in the morning," he said, so softly Susan wasn't even sure she'd heard right.

Far into the night, Susan went on waiting. Lying awake beside Robert in bed, she recalled news stories of bombs thrown through front windows into rooms such as this. For the first time, she understood fully the damage they did. There was really nothing at all, she saw now, between the person sleeping and the street. Outside, dogs barked and other dogs barked back. Moving nearer to Robert, she felt herself lulled by the steady rhythm of his breathing.

Early the next morning, Susan and Robert rode with Uncle Ben to the farm. It had never crossed Susan's mind that a person could be a farmer and still live in the suburbs. "If it were my farm, I'd sooner have my house right on it and not have to cart myself back and forth," Aunt Reesa had said, echoing Susan's own view.

The farm was much smaller than Susan had expected, who only knew pictures in books of Kansas wheat and Iowa corn fields, farms which swept the countryside and stretched as far as any eye could see. A Georgia farm, she saw now, could be taken in in one eyeful. Dressed in dungarees, a flannel shirt, and boots, Susan walked out to where half a dozen or so cows were penned. Others were grazing loose in the field. "They're none of them milking cows," Uncle Ben explained to her.

Susan reached out and touched the nearest one gently on the head. Unplanned, her fingers searched out the sledgehammer shaped place between its eyes, the spot she knew about from Robert. Long ago he had mentioned to her shooting a pig when he was a child on the farm, and she, thinking he was joking, had asked, did you shoot a cow too? A cow, he had explained then, was killed with a sledgehammer. Susan thought it over for weeks. Why, she finally asked, didn't you kill the pigs with a sledgehammer, too? That was when Robert had explained to her that there is no place on a pig's head like there is on a cow's, a place which Susan could see now seemed ready-made for a hammer blow. "Where do you keep the pigs?" she asked Uncle Ben.

The previous week she had watched a television special on the education channel. It was about wild boars. Susan had heard the narrator say that of all the interesting things to know about wild pigs, more interesting even than their foot-long tusks or versatile snouts, was that the male pig's sex organ was 18 inches long, with a corkscrew at its end that could be twirled around and around during mating. Susan, having explained about the program to Robert, had asked him if domestic pigs and wild pigs had everything the same. Robert, astonished by the question, had told her he had no idea.

"Last year," Uncle Ben informed Susan, "I kept one pig, but it's gone now." Susan wondered, but didn't ask, if he had shot it.

She followed him into the chicken house and picked some eggs. Collected, she would correct herself later on, telling about it. Afterward, she had an overwhelming urge to wash her hands. Her father, a dentist, had kept after Susan, all the time that she was growing up, to wash her hands and brush her teeth before and after everything she did. He had died two years before, and ever since Susan has frantically been doing both.

"A chicken will sometimes eat its own egg if it isn't col-lected up soon enough," Uncle Ben told Susan on the way home. Susan was surprised to hear it. "Well, not every chicken will do that," Uncle Ben said. "But the ones that do it will do it regularly." He also told her about a hired man on the farm when he was growing up who had gone to axe a chicken. The axe had slipped and hit a pole, bounced back and cut off that man's nose. "My mother, your husband's grandmother, picked up the nose from the dirt and sewed it right back on that hired man's face with the black thread she kept in a box for doctoring the animals."

Within days of returning to New York, Susan will borrow a library book on poultry, trying to discern the truth about hens and eggs, but it won't tell her what she wants to know. "Ferrets will sometimes steal chicken eggs," a fellow painter who grew up on a farm will inform her, trying to be helpful, when Susan asks.

* * *

Now, though, back at Uncle Ben's and Aunt Reesa's house, the first thing that Susan did was wash her hands and brush her teeth. Then she examined the rooms more carefully than she'd had time to do the night before. Aunt Reesa was glad to show her everything. The house was large, with high ceilings, and in each bedroom a kerosene stove was set in the middle of the floor, naturally unused in April. Looking closer, Susan saw that some of the school work on the walls was from decades ago, though some was recent, apparently done by grandchildren. On both sides of the living room fireplace was an antique doll collection, and quilts seemed everywhere. "They're beautiful," Susan told Aunt Reesa, who informed her she had made them all.

"One year I made thirty-four altogether," she said with some pride. Getting up, Aunt Reesa went into another room and came back holding a quilt with lots of red and green and gold. She unfolded it for Susan. "Here, you can have this one. The stitches are a little large," she explained without apologizing. "I made it the winter I had cataracts." Susan, pleased to have the quilt, was also interested in hearing more about the cataracts.

"Do you still have them?" she asked. Aunt Reesa did not. She had gone to the doctor when they got too bad, she told Susan. He had set her in his chair, put an egg cup on her eye and sucked them out. She didn't even require any bandage, though the doctor had advised her to wear dark glasses and avoid close work for several days after. Now, she said, she could see fine.

(On the same day that Susan borrows the library book about poultry, she'll also consult a reference book on cataracts. "Couching was practiced by the ancients," she'll read. "It consisted of dislocating the lens downward and backward into the vitreous chamber. The first mention of couching appears in records of Celsus, a Roman physician of the first century A.D. It persisted until the early 18th century." Learning this, Susan will reflect on what the chances are of its persisting still in

107

Georgia. Reading further, she'll discover that in addition to two modern forms of surgery, there exists a procedure known as phacoemulsification, relatively new, using an ultrasonic needle to suck out the cataract, and allowing the patient to return to all activities immediately afterward. The book warns, however, that it's a technique requiring utmost proficiency and therefore rarely done. Rarely done where, Susan will wonder. For all she knows, it's an everyday event in Georgia.)

Before heading back to the airport, Susan and Robert drove far out in to the country where Tineen, Uncle Ben's oldest daughter, lived with her husband Joel, and their nine children. Their home was a brick mansion Joel had built on acres of woodland that wasn't a farm. When he wasn't building, he taught math at the local high school. The house was very modern, filled with an abundance of objects and appliances whose possibilities Susan had never even considered. Concealed buttons in almost every room, when pressed, caused shelves to raise and lower, closets to open and shut, tape decks to emerge and put themselves away. There was a bedroom for each child with an adjoining bath. Several of their bedrooms contained computers. As in her mother's house, Tineen's walls were hung with photographs of relatives. She told Susan the name of each one. Naturally, some were of Tineen's children. Susan, who had often been dismayed by her own children's rudeness, was amazed how well-mannered Tineen's children were, except for the second from the baby, two year old Josephina, who, upon being left alone briefly in the room with Susan, took the occasion to attack the table leg with her teeth. Susan, who had once wanted a large family herself, had changed her mind after finding two a sufficient handful. Although she would willingly die for them, she hadn't been the least bit displeased when they left her for college. She regarded Josephina warily. A wild child, she thought, relieved when Tineen reappeared and offered to show her around the upstairs.

* * *

Riding to the airport, and then flying to New York, Susan quietly tried to absorb the weekend just past. As she'd expected, country living comprised depths that city life lacked. The lives she had seen seemed so much more authentic than her own. Beside them, hers seemed suddenly shallow, unneedfully solitary. Why then, she wondered, surprised and unprepared, was she looking forward with such pleasure to returning home, to her own sparse and sanitized apartment where children's school papers invariably had been filed in boxes almost as soon as they were handed back or, worse, thrown out, and photographs lay hidden inside albums or tucked away on closet shelves, and her sedentary cat would probably keel over dead one day of something like a heart attack?

"What are you thinking?" Robert asked.

"Maybe," Susan replied, "when we get home, I'll take some of the photographs out of the closet and have them framed to hang on the walls." Weeks went by, however, and the closest she got was to take them down and examine them, then wrap them up again and put them back. She did this on a night when Robert worked late.

When he came home, Susan asked: "How did you kill the mule?"

"I beg your pardon?" Robert answered, puzzled.

"On the farm?" said Susan. "How did you kill the mule on the farm?"

"We never did," said Robert, sounding genuinely horrified. "The mule pulled the plow. Why would we have killed him?"

"When he got too old," Susan persisted. "When he couldn't pull the plow anymore."

"When he got too old to pull the plow," said Robert, "we turned him out to graze. Besides," he added, "what would a person do with a dead mule anyway?"

Now, Susan had read more than a few stories in her life. As a child, in fact, she had read every fairy tale that she could get her hands on. She knew how many stories there were about mules—muleskins to be exact. There seemed no end to the number of tales in which a farmer, or field hand, or slave, walked through town calling: Muleskin for sale, muleskin for sale, what will you give for this muleskin for sale. Often, she reflected, the muleskin had been the point of the story. But she didn't mention all of this to Robert, at least not that night.

A few evenings later Susan attended an art exhibit. When she arrived home, Robert was in the living room, watching television, contemplating her cat.

"Tell me," he asked. "Has that cat of yours ever so much as set foot out of doors?"

Susan stared at her husband thoughtfully. He knew it never had. "Where would it go?" she inquired.

"Maybe it might just like a breath of fresh air," he said reasonably.

"Maybe it would," Susan agreed. That was when she told him about the muleskins in the stories. "Where do you think they got so many muleskins from in the first place?" she asked.

Robert smiled the smile that Susan loved so well, in which his mouth turned down instead of up. He pulled her onto his lap, smoothed back her hair the way he used to smooth their daughter Sara's. "Sometimes a mule will die of old age," he told her gently. "Did you ever think of that?" Then he pulled her close and kissed her. Sometime afterward, when Susan had time to think again, she didn't think of mules, or farms, or living in the city with a cat. She thought instead of Robert whom she had loved so many years, of their two grown children, and of her favorite lines from a Woody Allen film. In *The Purple Rose of Cairo*, Mia Farrow is describing her lover, a movie star who has stepped down from the screen to be by her side. "He's fictional," she explains. "But you can't have everything." Susan had liked the film, but Robert had thought it tedious and pointless.

Growing Pains

"But what I want to know is this," my son says in that tone of voice I hardly notice anymore. "Was the divorce because you were having an affair?"

I look at him, this child I hardly like of late. So that is what this year has been about. That he is sixteen now means I am thirty-three.

I do not answer right away. Why should I? His wanting to know tells me nothing by itself. "Why do you ask me such a question now?" I ask. What is it to you anyway, I think.

He looks at me with loathing. I can't remember when he looked at me with something less. I have tried to tell my sister what it's like living with him this way. "It's terrible," I say inadequately.

"But what exactly does he do?" she asks.

I try explaining. "It isn't what he does, but what he might do. It seems to me he might do anything." She waits, as though there must be more. I try again. "It's like living with a schizophrenic. There is nothing anyone could tell me that he's done that would surprise me."

"Oh," she says, not understanding. "Is that all? That's how adolescents are. They're crazy."

I wish I could believe her. She has three herself. "But this is different," I say, knowing she does not believe me.

Now, staring at him standing there, I see his father, whom

111

he hasn't seen since he was three. Wherever his father may be, and knowing him it could be China, or maybe just across the street, he looks like him, he speaks like him, he thinks like him. "Do you think so?" his grandmother asks, his father's mother. "I have always thought he looked like Joe." Joe is his father's older brother. "Don't be silly," my mother tells me. "You imagine things." What I truly think I do not say out loud. I truly think that I am raising someone else's child. It horrifies me.

"All right, don't tell me. I'll find out myself," he says, and interrupts my thoughts. "I have a right to know," he shouts, slamming out the door.

I am unsurprised. Children nowadays have every right. "You have no rights. In my house are just the privileges I give you." That was my mother telling me. If I had not picked up this child every time he cried, would he be the same today?

Today is Thursday. I do not go to work. In return for working Saturdays, I have every Thursday off. I like it that way. I heat a pot of water to make tea.

I would not have heard this question I just heard, I tell myself, had I not allowed my son to visit with his grandmother on his father's side. I suppose I didn't have to let him. But she is an old woman with just one leg. I did not have the heart to tell her no. I wonder now what she has told him.

Considering her age and her condition, his grandmother is remarkably agile. When indoors, she hops about from room to room on her one leg, assisted by a pair of crutches. Outside, she uses a prosthesis that has never fit. She will not use a wheelchair, and I do not blame her for that. "Please," she used to beg when her husband was alive. "Don't make me use the wheelchair." And he would lift her up and set her in it. "Don't be foolish," he would say.

I like to think about the way she lost her leg. It reconfirms for me what I have often said about my former husband and his family: They're all peculiar. Whether what I've often said is true, I have no way of knowing.

She lost her leg sitting down and laying it across a railroad track before the train came. Angry at her husband, she meant to lay herself across it, but at the last moment lost her courage and pulled back. I'll show him he cannot treat me as he does and get away with it, she must have thought. He didn't, either. "I have a cripple for a wife," he'd say afterward, bitter, to anyone who'd listen. He hadn't been entirely unprepared though. When he was eighteen he'd come home one day to find his mother dead, her head stuck in the oven. It was her third and most successful try. I ask myself, was this woman's husband, who also was *my* husband's grandfather, like my husband's father then, and also like my husband? Did she put her head inside the oven to escape her spouse, or was she withdrawing from her son who is the grandfather of my son who hates me? Is it an inherited condition, or how we raise them? Or is it just that all of them are men? Or did I make it up? My son has asked his grandmother about her leg, but she doesn't seem to remember what I do.

"An accident," she told him. "One of those unlucky things. It was rush hour. I stood too near the track. A young man in a hurry bumped me. Thank God it was just my leg and not my life." There's proof on my side, though. She never sued the railroad or the man. Of course, I too have never sued, never sued her son to help support her grandson. Perhaps we're simply not litigious people, or we do not make our indiscretions public, or we aren't up to seeing our actions through to their conclusions.

I fix myself a cup of tea. *What to Tell the Children When You're Getting a Divorce.* Tell them everything. Tell them only what they need to know. Just tell the truth. Working in a library as I do, I used to look for help in books. I sneaked them out inside my coat, then sneaked them in again. I have frequently been amazed, hearing people say out loud the books they want to read. "Have you anything on marital dysfunction?" I once was asked.

None of the books that I took home to read to my son had anything to do with us. *Having divorced parents means having two homes and two families. It means having two Christmas trees,* said one picture book. When my son remembers what was good about that time, he remembers sitting on the floor and eating from a trunk. "Pretend that it's a picnic," I said gaily.

I have no memories of that juncture. I have carefully nurtured blankness. Except for one eidetic image that remains: of him driving away in the snow, everything we owned piled around him in the car. He took the car, the cat, and my guitar, overflowing the U-Haul that he hauled behind. He looked as he did when I first met him. He was singing. He often sang to himself. You couldn't tell his mood from what he sang. It was just something that he did. On the rare occasions when I have tried to tell his son what was good about his father, I have told him that: "That man could sing."

"Then why did you leave him?"

"There is more to life than singing," I say.

"Is that really why?" he asks.

"Sure," I answer, who have rarely known why anything. I think I left for the same reason I first went. I was afraid to be alone.

But marriage wasn't quite what I'd envisioned. A singing salesman, my husband was always on the road. He sold anything. Nor was he at all reticent about his trips and what he did on them. He told me everything. "But you're the only one I love," he told me.

That's when I started working at the library. Anyone who thinks a library is not a good place for meeting new people, has never worked in one. "You owe a dollar fifty," I told a man with large, long-fingered hands. Then, looking up, I saw that he was laughing at me. Later, when I went to start my car it wouldn't start. He fiddled with some wires and it ran.

"Can I buy you a cup of coffee?" he offered. I accepted out of gratitude.

When my husband came back from his selling trip that time, I was allergic to him. When he touched me, I got hives. *Hives that come like that are caused by something else,* I read not long ago—*his soap, his after shave, his starch.* I was not allergic to his soap, his after shave, his starch. I couldn't bear for him to touch me. "Women learn to bear these things," his mother told me. It was the same thing she had said when he told her I didn't want to have intercourse with him my first day home from the hospital having had his son.

"It hurts," I told the doctor at my six-week check-up.

"You're not supposed to do it yet," he told me. He didn't tell me, though, what to do about not doing it. "I know more than you about these things," my husband said. He was twenty-six to my just seventeen. Sometimes I think my distaste for him started then. *A hormone imbalance will cause the tissues to lose their elasticity causing pain during intercourse*, I read in a library book last month. Would knowing that have saved my marriage?

All day I consider what to tell my son. I look in closets, and peruse old letters. I am not sure what I'm searching for. Late in the afternoon it comes to me. I can tell him anything. I wonder why I never thought of that before. I blame the books. None of them so much as mentioned it.

I reread my letters carefully. I see now that I've saved them for a reason. I rearrange and sort them. I have always saved selectively. In my mind I annotate the letters, like notes in books explaining what is missing. Now it all makes sense. It's a story anyone could easily believe. I believe it.

"Sit down," I say to him when he comes home that night. "Sit down and be quiet. For once in your life, listen to me. I will do the talking." I do. I thrust letters at him. I explain the voids. I tell him who was right and who was wrong. I tell him sometimes there are not two sides to every story. I tell him, which is true, that I have never lied to him. He can believe me now or not. *I am sorry*, his father wrote me once, rebounding from a sad affair. *You were altogether right and I was wrong. I would do anything to change what's been.* If his father thought that was the truth, who am I to change it.

A week or so later I see my son outside on the lawn snapping a bullwhip, at first experimentally, after a while expertly, taking off the heads of dandelions. I have not the least idea where he has found the bullwhip. Every afternoon for the next few months when he is not at work, or hanging out at the garage, he is out there on the lawn practicing. What is he practicing for? Finally, he puts away the bullwhip, or he sells it, or he gives it to a friend.

I hear from someone, not from him, maybe his grandmother told me during one of our rare telephone conversations, that his father was in town. Not was, had been. Had been in town and telephoned his son. Of course he would have liked to see him, but he was on a selling trip, this time a toy convention. Next time they'd have lunch.

I hear the lock turn in the door now, and he is in the room. Outside, snow is falling. "What's for dinner, Marmalade?" he asks. He hasn't called me by that nickname now in years. It must mean something. I hope it means the worst is over. "Pepper steak," I say, standing up to start our dinner. I'm glad that I told him what I did, or that he is getting over adolescence, or that his father didn't have time for lunch.

I glance at him over my shoulder as I fry a Spanish onion. He is singing to himself. I think again how much he's like his father, as his father was like his. This last my mother pointed out to me. I disbelieved her at the time from habit.

"You imagine things," I told her.

These Things Can Happen

"So, how did you and Vergil meet?" It surprises me how often I'm still asked that question.

"Before we were born our feet were tied together with a piece of invisible red string," is my favorite answer. Borrowed from Chinese folklore, it is short and to the point, much simpler than trying to explain the circumstances: Ages ago, back in the sixties, I lived in the apartment under his, and his bathtub leaked. Of course that's only a detail. Knowing why I lived there in the first place goes further to illuminate the heart of our relationship. My presence was not a matter of choice on my part, unless one considers a lack of reasonable alternatives the same as making a decision.

A friend of mine was being transferred by her company to California for a year. The apartment was hers. "I'd consider it a favor if you stayed in it," she told me. "Plus it will give you time to get yourself together." She meant get over my divorce from Henry.

I married Henry when I was seventeen. He was twenty-seven, a captain in the army. Reasonably tall, he had dark eyes, a sensual mouth, and the most perfect teeth I had ever seen. His uniforms were sharply pressed and his black shoes glistened, always. He swept my mother off her feet. Why else did she encourage me to marry him? I do not believe she ever actually said this in so many words but, nevertheless, it was what I heard: "You may never get another offer this good, not even close. You'd better jump at the chance."

At least two good things came from that marriage: Henry paid for me to go to college, and I got to travel. He was stationed in Europe. My mother warned me: "You want to be careful. Europeans are anti-Semitic." But almost everywhere I went, I was taken for French. "American," I'd say, crossing this border or that. "I'm from New York." "Oui, Madame," they'd answer. "Ou allez-vous?" In the south of France I saw why. Women there looked like me: small, slim, with dark hair and pale skin. Europeans, I thought, are easily fooled. Back in New York, I told my mother.

"Don't be silly," she said. "Your nose is a dead giveaway. Probably they were trying to trick you."

Vergil does not understand that part of my life. "Yes," he has said, perplexed. "But you were still a child. Where was your father at the time?"

It is a good question. Where he generally was, I suppose: in his drugstore.

"Pharmacy. Your father is a pharmacist," our mother corrected us.

He often took me with him to the store. By age four, I could roll pennies and line up cigarettes. There were not that many brands: Camels, Old Golds, Philip Morris, Parliament, Lucky Strike. King Size was just coming in. To the rear of the store was the room where he mixed medicines. There were shelves of labeled bottles, rows of tins and vials. He showed me how to weigh out colored powder onto white paper, forming little hills, then pull apart empty gelatin capsules and tamp the open narrow ends against the powder until they were full. Finally, I'd reclose the capsules. I pretended I was a pharmacist.

Behind the prescription department was an even smaller room, lit by a single bulb suspended from the ceiling, with a pull chain to turn it on and off. It contained a desk and a chair. Here was where Daddy sat when business was slow, and ate sugared pastries and listened to classical music on the radio.

When I was there, standing or leaning against a corner of the chair, I ate and listened with him.

My mother did not care to hear the radio. Daddy seldom turned his on when he was home, and when he did he played it low. Sometimes, I'd pass by when the door to their bedroom was ajar, and look in. I'd see him stretched across the double bed, his eyes closed, his glasses on the night table beside him, nodding along with the music.

For the most part, though, he was in his store, seven days a week from early morning until late at night, except Sundays when he closed at two. He didn't actually have to be there every minute that the store was open. He employed two other full-time pharmacists, and when business was good, sometimes three. Often I helped, too, after school and on weekends. "Poor Daddy," Mother used to say frequently, referring to his hours.

I do not hold my parents entirely to blame for my first marriage. They only reflected the mores they knew. Both of my grandmothers were barely fourteen when they married. Despite this, my mother had managed to put off her own marriage until her late thirties, so by the time she wed Daddy, her family had given up on her and were resigned to her being an old maid. Even in our neighborhood, an enclave of identical brick houses in Queens, to which we'd moved from Manhattan when my sister Claudia and I still were in grade school, it was common knowledge that by age twenty a girl's chances for matrimony declined by geometric progression with each passing year. Our parents did not say that to us. They didn't have to. We heard it from girlfriends who heard it, usually from their fathers, and repeated it. Where did their fathers get this information? Why did we believe it?

We didn't believe it. "Who cares?" we said bravely. "Of course they are wrong"—then jumped at the first man to come along. I jumped first. Claudia jumped right behind me, marrying Gerald the following year. "A college professor is almost as good as a physician," our mother told her. "So he'll never get rich but the hours are better."

"I do hold her responsible," Claudia has said to me through the years. But at the time, she only said, "Some parents would not allow a younger sister to get married first." That was the truth.

Since then, our mother's changed her mind about some things. She tells her grandchildren, for instance, "It's as easy to fall in love with somebody rich as somebody poor. Take your time. Look around. It isn't good to get married too young."

"You never told us that," Claudia and I say to her, accusingly.

"So sue me," she tells us back. "I'm older now. I know more."

Perhaps I should have mentioned this to begin with: Our mother is a lawyer. Not knowing that, I realize, can create an erroneous impression. On the other hand, knowing too much can do the same.

I once showed a photograph of my mother to a woman at work. "Your mother is so small," she said, sounding surprised, turning the photograph this way and that. "Hearing you talk about her, I always pictured her as large."

"My mother?" I took back the picture and examined it. "No," I said. "She has always been a small person, short and somewhat chubby."

The reason I so seldom mention my mother's occupation is, I think, because it's been so little use to me, none. When I was getting my divorce, having a lawyer for a mother didn't help me. Nor was it of any help when Vergil's bathtub leaked soapy water into mine, and I couldn't get anyone to fix it. A plumber in the family might have come in handy then.

I made threatening phone calls, sent letters, finally went to the management office myself. "It's disgusting," I told the woman with thin straw-colored hair and no-color eyes who sat at the desk. She stared at me for several seconds, then said, "I understand." I took it to mean she'd do something about it.

Have it repaired, for instance. Of course she didn't. Perhaps from the start she meant only that she agreed with me. Well, who wouldn't? Someone else's used bath water in my tub, after all.

Weeks passed. I went upstairs. "I realize it isn't your fault," I said, explaining my problem at the open door, staring down at my feet. "But if you complain, also, perhaps it will help."

I looked up. The man looking down at me was thin-set and black. He had a gold front tooth that glinted as he smiled. I'd never known anyone with a gold tooth, though of course I'd seen pictures in books of people who had them.

"How terrible," he said, his expression half amused and half concerned. "Certainly, I'll lodge a complaint."

Having thanked him, I prattled on. "It's a good thing I have a second bathroom," I said. This was probably an effort on my part to avoid the appearance of intimacy, or impropriety. I'm sure it had nothing to do with his blackness. Still, I didn't repeat what I'd said to the rabbity woman in the management office.

Months went by before Vergil told me what he'd thought at the time. "You were so small. You looked so young. At first I thought you were the teen-age daughter of the family under me, sent as an emissary."

Young? I was twenty-two by then. I was in graduate school and worked part-time in the college library. I was a married woman, nearly divorced. I felt altogether grown up. Almost every week official papers came to me in batches, by registered mail, documents pertaining to divorce, usually concerning money that was Henry's and which he meant to keep that way. They all required my notarized signature. Both my parents were notaries. I could have gone to them. But I preferred going to banks or travel agencies instead. Each time I found someplace new where I hadn't been before, and paid the going rate, in quarters.

Vergil remembers more: "You were barefoot, skinny, you

looked so determined. It was a little hard to make you out under all that hair. But after you left I did consider what it might be like to take a bath with you," he says in his teasing voice. "I thought about soaping your skin, drying you off, combing out thousands of strands of silk hair."

By the time he tells me this, we have taken more baths together than I have tried to count, and made love both in and out of water. Each time we do, it seems to me brand new, and each time I feel I am drowning, or in danger of it. Yet, always and at the same time, I feel buoyed and safe, absolutely, as I have never felt before. How can a person feel both ways at once?

I think of the seal woman in the Scottish folk tale whose sealskin was stolen. Her only choice then is to go home with the thief and live where he lives in his house on the beach. Time passes. She marries the man. Their life goes well enough, but often she sits by herself and stares out to sea. One day, when the man goes to town, he forgets to take the key to his strongbox from under his pillow. The woman finds the key, and unlocks the box. Her sealskin is in it. When the man returns, the box is open and his wife and the sealskin both are gone. She's put it on and flung herself into the sea. When Vergil makes love to me, I feel as that woman must have felt back in salt water. I feel I'm finally where I belong, at home in my own true element. All this comes later, though, long after the leaking bathtub has been fixed, and I no longer live beneath it anyway.

Getting it fixed was a job. I sent streams of letters by registered mail to: the management, the mayor, the Board of Health, authorities in Albany, my representatives in Congress. My mother encouraged me. "It's the only way," she said. Of course it wasn't. She could have written on her legal letterhead. Things might have happened sooner. She didn't suggest it.

Even so, plumbers eventually came. They made a hole in

my ceiling and replaced portions of the pipe. They left the hole, and went away. "We have to be sure the leak has stopped before we close it up," they told me.

I could see then that the tub itself was supported by heavy wooden beams, and in no danger of actually falling as I had originally feared. Though I could not see into the bathroom above me, I could hear every sound. I came to feel I was sharing my most private room with a stranger. The stranger sang as he showered and hummed while he shaved. His taste was eclectic: patriotic songs, religious hymns, even poetry was not beyond him. I used my other bathroom, except when I forgot or was in a hurry, and the one in disrepair was closer. Months passed before the plasterers came back and closed up my ceiling. The plaster dried, the painters painted, and I was alone in my apartment again.

If I felt lonely all those months I lived there on my own, I don't recall it. I went to school, I had a job, there were people whom I knew. If I missed sexual encounters, I don't recall that either. My only experience had been with Henry. If that was all there was to sex, I could forgo it without regret. The women's magazines my mother read included articles for women like me, on *solitary sexual behavior*. They called it *self-pleasuring*, and recommended it. One feminist went so far as to call it *our primary sex life*. "It is the sexual base, everything we do beyond that is simply how we choose to socialize our sex life," she said. I could not see it for myself. It seemed to me to miss the point, like pedaling an exercise bicycle or practicing piano on a painted keyboard.

Nor was that all. Vibrators were advertised, and sold through the mail, as well as in fashionable stores. Their discreet designs gave no hint of their possible sexual utility. "The sensual high that can be produced with the vibrator is fast, pleasurable, and reliable," promised one ad, as though a buyer's primary consideration was saving time.

Still, I must have been missing something. Good company, perhaps? Or conversation? Maybe just someplace nice to go, dressed up and in high-heeled shoes. Whatever it was, when

Vergil rang my doorbell, I was ready. But for what? He suggested dinner out— "To celebrate the fixing of the leaking tub."

Rubbing one bare foot against the other, I deliberated. It sounded better than studying for finals. Besides, if I refused he might think that I was prejudiced.

"Yes," I said. "Dinner would be lovely. I need just fifteen minutes to get dressed." That was the start. We dined out the rest of the week, and after that began eating in. We took turns cooking, and cleaned up together. We stayed up late and talked.

I start to say we talked about ourselves, but the truth is, mostly I talked about myself. That Vergil was an aeronautical engineer was probably the most personal thing he told me. Why, then, did I believe I knew so much about him? Why do I, sometimes, even think that now? And how was it that I came to be so much in love with him? What is it that gets into us, and takes over?

Certainly there is the matter of proximity. But why this particular man, then, and not that one? Surely physical appearance plays only a small part, and even sex comes after the fact. Those whom we love we're predisposed to find beautiful; and sex, however good, only confirms the original attraction. What then? I think perhaps it has to do with this: the way a lover sees himself, and how he sees himself in relationship to others.

Vergil saw himself as someone I could love. About that, there was no question. Even beyond that, though, was Vergil's image of himself in the world. People meeting him for the first time are frequently impressed by what they take for courtesy. It seems to me they may be missing the point, perhaps in much the same way as I have seen eloquence taken for meaning. I think what they're experiencing, and have no name for, is Vergil's view of himself, entirely whole and rational, extended to encompass them, and everyone. I believe for a woman to encounter such recognition in a man may be so rare that, when she does, she risks mistaking it for love. It confused me at first. Seeing Vergil with other women, I worried.

"How do I know how you feel about me if you act the same toward everyone?" I asked. "How do I know how you feel about them? And how can *they* tell?" In the context of my queries, it was clear that my pronouns were feminine. Did I calculate, deliberately, the effect of such questions? Was I seeking some declaration on his part? I wouldn't put it past me. Whatever my purpose, this was the result: From across the room, Vergil focused his eyes on mine and held them there. Anything he may have said, I don't remember. I recall instead a magnifying glass I once had. My father had given it to me when I was eight or nine. He had shown me how to use it to concentrate the rays of the sun onto scraps of white paper, then hold them there until the paper caught fire and burned.

When Vergil stood, crossed the room to where I sat, and took me in his arms, I felt like that. In slow motion, he undressed me, told me I was beautiful, carried me into the bedroom, and laid me on the bed. We were like players in some old-time melodrama. Even then, he would have left. That is his way and some part of his charm as a lover. Desire has often seemed strongest on my part. It was years before I understood fully that what we began that night was his idea from the start.

"Don't go," I begged him. "Stay with me. Come to bed."

"What do you know?" he said. "You're still almost a child. If I come now, I will come forever."

"Yes," I said. "Fine."

"Come," he said then. "You are mine." And I did, and I do, and I am.

Several weeks after Vergil and I became lovers I had a dream in which a large and beautiful red and gold rooster flew through my window. I fed it, and it stayed. It was mine from then on. It came and it went, but it always returned to me at night. Because it was so beautiful, I worried someone would steal it. But no one except me seemed to want it. When I awoke, I was surprised and pleased to have had such a dream. A week or so later, at work, I came across the information that for centuries, especially in certain Eastern countries, the rooster was considered an erotic symbol.

Eventually, I told my mother everything. "I think I'm in love," I told her. My mother was horrified. Though her reaction was not entirely unpredictable, I was somewhat taken by surprise. She had always prided herself on being a liberal thinker.

"Couldn't you just go away with him somewhere for a weekend? Get it out of your system?" Did my mother truly say this, or do I only imagine that she did? Certainly it wasn't out of the question. She did, at that time, encourage me to go away for weekends with men who asked me, who I hardly knew, men who had sailboats and campers. "It's for your own good," my mother insisted. "You want to get married again." I wasn't sure that was so. My marriage to Henry was all I had to go by.

My father's response was, perhaps, more predictable. He had no political leanings. He simply stopped talking to me. The difference between Daddy talking to me and Daddy not talking to me was not always discernible.

Briefly, and at my mother's urging, Henry stepped back into my life. Our divorce was final by then. "Your mother's only thinking of what's best for you," he said. "You're making a mistake. I've known men like that. He'll leave you in a minute, be gone like a flash. Believe me, you cannot trust such a person." Did he mean I could not trust any black man? Any man? Or just Vergil?

I received a letter from my friend in California. Her year out there was almost up. She wrote to say that she'd decided to stay on, and wouldn't be renewing her New York lease. Given my financial situation, I knew trying to rent an apartment on my own would be useless.

"Where will you go? What will you do?" My mother asked me that. She didn't say: Come home, sort out your life, you're still so young. "If you play your cards right, I'm sure in no time at all you'll be married again," she said. Naturally, she didn't mean to Vergil.

"But he's the one I love," I told her.

My mother shook her head. "Listen to me. I'm going to tell you a story. It really happened," she said. "I heard it from Sam Kane, a lawyer I know from way back. Sam's grandmother was Jewish. She married a man who was gentile. They had five children. Now and then, her husband left her. The last time he did, he was gone twenty years. When he returned he was an old man. Sam's grandmother took him back. Who knows why? Maybe from habit, or because he was family, or just because the children were grown and she didn't like living alone. Whatever her reason, that was that. Not too many years later, he had a heart attack and died.

"The oldest of their five children was Sam's father. He received a letter from a woman in Seattle. She had come across the obituary in a newspaper. She was trying to track down her own father and was contacting whoever she could find with his same name, or one that was similar. I don't know the details of her letter but, apparently, it was sufficiently unsettling that Sam's father never said a word to anyone about it, and never wrote back to the woman, probably not wanting to cause his own mother any further distress. Nevertheless, he did not throw out the letter. He put it in a strongbox for safekeeping, along with other papers. When he died, Sam inherited the box. He figured for his father to have kept the letter so long, it must have meant something to him. By then, Sam's grandmother was dead and there was no one left to hurt. Sam was going to Seattle on a business trip. He looked up the woman who had sent the letter, and telephoned her. She invited him to come and see her. He went. It turned out Sam's grandfather and the woman's father were one and the same. The woman told Sam how her father used to disappear for years at a time. No one knew where he went.

Every time he came back her mother took him in. They had four children. The woman had always believed her mother did it for their sake."

"Why are you telling me this?" I asked my mother.

"Wait, there's more. This isn't the end," she said. "The two families decided to get together. It turned out they liked one another, and all of them got along. Every year after that, they held a family reunion. A cousin of the woman from Seattle, who lived in Oregon, was so impressed that she told a friend, and also showed the friend a snapshot of her Washington cousin and the cousin's parents. 'Oh my God,' the friend said, and turned pale. 'That's my uncle Fred.' Fred," my mother said, "turned out to be Sam's same disappearing grandfather with a third family and a different first name." My mother looked at me, triumphantly. "See," she said.

"See what?"

"These things can happen. You should listen to me. I know what I'm saying, mixed marriages don't work."

The next week I packed my books, my food, my clothes, and moved upstairs.

"You're making a mistake," my mother warned. "Believe me: it will never last."

He's Sorry, She's Sorry, They're Sorry, Too

Sorelle stands, frowning, in the middle of her cluttered kitchen, in the apartment that they can't afford, in a suburb north of Baltimore. She has just hung up the telephone, for the second time this morning. It is Saturday and barely nine o'clock. Her first conversation was with Lily, her husband's grandmother; her next was with Johanna, his father's second wife. Weston, her husband, is not at home. Where he is, is anybody's guess.

Sorelle is tall and slim, and presents to the outer world a sense of inner calm she rarely feels. She is black, like everybody else in this story, except for Johanna, who is Jewish, and who is also from the country that was once called Rhodesia. So light of skin are some of them, however, that it almost passes belief, at least Johanna's belief, to hear them called black. Sorelle is almost, but not quite, that light. Her skin is smooth-textured and clear toned; it glints with hints of gold, and Johanna sometimes reflects on the time and the money white people will spend to affect precisely that look.

Before they ever met, Sorelle had been prepared to dislike Johanna, but afterward had changed her mind. Having never known anyone Jewish before, she sometimes wonders now if it is Johanna's religion that accounts for her sympathetic attitude, at least toward Sorelle and her increasingly frequent catastrophes. Not that Johanna is religious. So far as Sorelle is

129

aware, she does not even belong to any church (she means synagogue) or ever go to services. Or, perhaps, it is the other way around: Johanna's Jewishness accounting for Sorelle's sympathetic friendliness, her willingness to overlook the fact of Johanna's whiteness, and also her country of origin.

Their conversation this morning started out like this: How are you? How are the children? While Sorelle was answering "fine" to everything, she kept her eyes on Alessandria and Victoria, ages four and two, who were tumbling about in the living room. Last week Alessandria had been diagnosed as anemic; the iron pills she is supposed to take for it have made her constipated. The baby is running a fever, either from a slight cold, or a new tooth, or both.

But that's not why Sorelle had called. Her car is being repossessed. Again. This time by Weston's grandmother, Lily. Sorelle was hoping that Leon, Weston's father, would do something about it. When he wasn't home, Sorelle tried to find the right tone in which to tell Johanna. Now, standing in her kitchen, biting her bottom lip, Sorelle wonders why she bothered. Johanna had been of no help whatsoever.

This is Sorelle's situation: She'd been awakened at seven by Lily, calling to inform her that as of yesterday Sorelle had missed three car payments. Sorelle, who of course already knew that, had a plan. Now she has instructions. Lily has told her to pack up her children, put them in the car, and drive five hours south, past Petersburg, to where Lily lives, alone, in a huge house. Once there, Sorelle believes, with reason, that she will be directed to park the car, two years old with no extras (not even an arm on the door with which to pull it shut), in the large circular driveway that cuts a swath across the well kept lawn, alongside several other more resplendent cars, Lily's custom built Mercedes, for instance, and told to leave it there. How she then gets back home with the two children she presumes will be her own business. "What can Lily be thinking of?" Sorelle had asked Johanna on the telephone.

"Where is Wes?" Johanna replied in her reasonable way. Well, she wasn't the one being asked to undertake this journey.

Sorelle repeated what she'd said earlier to Lily, that she had no idea. Johanna wished that she could think of something useful to suggest. "Dad should be back soon," she finally said, vaguely, meaning Leon of course.

Sorelle starts making peanut butter sandwiches to take on the trip, and smiles with no pleasure. She recalls her oldest brother's nickname for her. "Sorry," Rupert called her when she was growing up. It's turning out to be the truth. She's starting to believe she made a sorry choice getting mixed up with this family in the first place. Rupert has turned out to be a better fortuneteller than their mom, who does it for a living. "Don't let that boy get by you," she had warned Sorelle. "Some folks don't know a gold mine when they see one." She couldn't have meant Weston. She must have meant his family. "What's wrong with that boy?" his relatives ask whenever they're together. They mean, what's wrong with him that he never finished college; everybody else has. Well, Sorelle's mother might not have noticed. Had Sorelle continued on past high school, she'd have been the first one in the family ever to do that.

Sorelle puts the sandwiches into a brown paper bag along with some cookies, and leaves the kitchen as it is. She winds a scarf around her head, tacking down abundant hair, pulls on her boots, and dresses the children for going out of doors; she packs an extra change of clothes for them, just in case. (In case what?) If Sorelle knew of some other choice, she'd make it. Sometimes she thinks of giving up, like now for instance. But she doesn't know how. Give up, and then do what? she wonders.

On the way out the door she remembers that old children's game they used to play: We are going on a trip to grandmother's house. I will take an apple.

"We are going to great-grandmother's house," Sorelle tells her children. "I will take Alessandria. Alessandria will take her blanket," she croons. "We will go together in the car." This is when she sees that, for the first time in her life, the point of making a trip is taking the car. "It's a long way from Alessandria to Victoria," she says to her children as though it's a game, but what she's really thinking is how far a distance back it is from Petersburg to Baltimore.

In the alcove that serves as a dining room in their condominium in Great Neck, Johanna dawdles over her third cup of coffee, cold. She is still in her night clothes. A long cashmere robe with quilted collar and cuffs is haphazardly tied around her. Johanna is in her middle forties, slender, with dark eyes, and dark hair she pulls back into a bun, or wears twisted and held with silver combs that Leon buys as birthday, Christmas, I've-been-gone-on-a-business-trip presents for her. Gray strands have begun appearing here and there this year, and though Johanna regrets them, it is unlikely she will ever color them. As time passes, she will even come to like their silvery look among the black strands. Her expression is generally serious, scholarly; when she smiles, it is like sun breaking through clouds. At the moment, she is frowning. The calf of her right leg rests across a corner of the tabletop, her bare foot hangs over its edge, a habit she tries not to indulge when Leon is home. Until Sorelle's telephone call, she was enjoying her leisure. She is several weeks into an eighteen-month sabbatical taken from her job as a textile conservator in the costumes department of New York's Metropolitan Museum of Art. Already she's begun using the time to work on designs of her own. Now, though, she concentrates on Sorelle's most current calamity. Johanna loves Sorelle. As one given to understatement she often says, "I am so fond of that child," but what she means by it is what most other people mean when they say "love." What *can* Lily be thinking of? she asks herself.

Johanna remembers life when Rebecca, Leon's child and hers, was a baby. Rebecca is away at college now. That Lily would actually have Sorelle pack up her children and drive so many miles surpasses Johanna's understanding. That Lily will actually reclaim the car and send Sorelle and the two children home on the bus is not something Johanna believes will actually happen. But what purpose could be served then by the journey? Johanna wishes Leon had been home to take the call.

It is not the first time she has had this wish. She wishes it, for instance, when any of the children call with a crisis. "Is Dad there?" they ask. Eugenia, Weston's older sister, asks it; Weston asks it; and so, too, does Rebecca. Well Sorelle asks it, too, but when he isn't, unlike the others, she will tell Johanna her problems, though sympathy is all Johanna ever seems to have to offer. When Sorelle's car was repossessed last year, Leon was away and Johanna knew it first. It wasn't until Weston called Lily, though, that help was forthcoming. That was how Lily came to hold her current lien on the car.

"Perhaps you misunderstood what she meant," Johanna had started to say this time, but stopped herself. When Lily wants a thing done, she is very clear on who, and how, and when. Johanna believes this is one reason Lily's own children have contrived through the years to keep their distance. If Sorelle believes that Lily is expecting her to put the children in the car today and drive from Baltimore to Petersburg to give the car away, Johanna would be prepared to bet her life that that's what Lily meant. On the other hand, Johanna also knows it's possible that by the time Sorelle arrives, Lily may have changed her mind. Johanna continues sitting at the table. If there is something she can do to help, she can't imagine what.

Along I-95 there is nothing of interest to see, and traffic slows to a crawl, periodically, for no apparent reason. Sorelle, driving, glances over her shoulder, sees both children sleeping in their car seats in the back. There are cookie crumbs around their mouths. Her children always seem sticky to her, no matter how often she wipes their hands and their faces.

No matter, also, how carefully she braids and ties up their hair, by the time they get wherever they are going Alessandria's, at least, will have come partially undone. She will have pulled her jacket hood on and off her head enough times, or rolled herself across a floor, or rubbed her hair against a wall, or failing all of that, she will grab wisps of it in her own small fists and pull upward from the roots. She has started to develop bald spots here and there from doing this, though in all other ways she seems a well-adjusted child. People often stop to admire both her and her sister, and it is true, sticky or not, they are exceptionally attractive children. Whichever parent they took after, it could not have hurt their looks. "Such a handsome couple," people say when they see Weston and Sorelle together.

Alessandria snores gently in back. Even their sleeping, Sorelle thinks, is something Weston's family holds against her. "Children with regular bedtimes," they tell her regularly, "get up in the morning." Hers have to be dragged from their beds, protesting. It is useless for Sorelle to explain that by the time she leaves work, picks one up from day care, the other from her sitter, makes dinner, straightens the house, and gives baths, it is already late. They'd all worked, too, even Johanna had a full-time job, when their children were young. None of them recall babies who stayed up after dark. Johanna is commiserative, as usual, but only Sorelle's own mother, and her sisters, understand. Well, Sorelle thinks, wouldn't they have to?

Sorelle's mother is a spiritualist, a medium who sees the future and can tell the past. That's what her fliers say. As a child, Sorelle's job had been to stand outside, on the crowded Philadelphia street where they lived, and hand them out, encouraging new customers. Such a sweet-looking little girl, people would think, passing by. Women were not afraid to follow Sorelle up a flight of stairs into a stranger's house where she would lead them to the curtained-off corner in the large front room and point to the folding chair. "Hold out your hands," Sorelle's mother would tell them. "Did you enjoy your reading?" Sorelle always asked, politely, when they came back down the stairs, solitary figures cast in street lights and shadows.

Sorelle recalls the one time Johanna had met her mother and had her fortune told. "You can ask me questions now," her mother said when she was finished, as she always did. Johanna, who'd never had her fortune told before, was at a loss. She asked the only question she could think of: "Do you like to read?" She meant, do you like to read books? because if Sorelle's mother did, then Johanna knew one to recommend about a fortuneteller. *Searching for Caleb* was the one she had in mind. Right away she saw it was the wrong question. Hadn't Sorelle's mother just read, Johanna's palms for instance? Didn't she do it for a living: tea leaves, cards, conjure roots, astrological signs?

"Probably she wanted to send you something to thank you for telling her fortune," Sorelle said later to her mother, smoothing the afternoon over, placating her mother's feelings. "She always sends books."

"Well, a foreigner," Sorelle's mother said, willing to be pacified for Sorelle's sake, her tone indicating how little she expected of such people in general.

Johanna frequently does send books, to Sorelle: new books, used books, cherished books from her own collection. They arrive every few weeks in large brown envelopes. It was this about Sorelle, finding out she was a reader, that drew Johanna to her from the start. "You should have gone to college," Johanna once told her. But Sorelle's own mother had never seen that in her daughter's future. "Be a beautician like your sister," she said. She meant like Editha who worked in a mortuary, fixing dead people's hair. "The pay's good, and they don't talk back," Editha boasted.

Johanna, though, who cannot conceive of life without books, believes that it is Sorelle's reading which has nourished her life and made it possible for her to fit into Weston's family as well as she does. What Johanna does not understand is that while Sorelle is grateful for the books she sends, and flattered by Johanna's judgment of her interest in them, and her ability to read them, she is sometimes also resentful. Some books have been beyond her; in general, though, it is a question of quantity and not of subject. Sorelle is already up late every night seeing to Alessandria and Victoria. She hasn't the time that Johanna seems to demand of her for reading. Also, there is the matter of the books which Johanna sends the children, intending for them to be read to nightly. Some nights Sorelle is simply too tired, or the children are; or Weston is home and the television is going and the children both fidget, and will not attend to her reading. "Weston should read to them, too," Johanna has advised. Sorelle lets it pass, which Johanna takes for agreement.

Though Sorelle doesn't show it, increasingly she feels herself not quite up to the life that circumstances have provided her. Though Weston is frequently "between jobs," as he is now, and their refrigerator often empty, and their rent regularly overdue, their life is acted out on a grand scale, or what passes for one to Sorelle. When Weston is among relatives, for instance, and sometimes even when he isn't, Sorelle will be surprised to hear him talk of taxes, politics, real estate, as if he had some stake in them. Rarely, she will gather courage and point out to him he doesn't. "Of course he doesn't," Leon says whenever he is present and his son's activities come up. "Someone who never finished college!" Then he'll add, more often than not, "He shouldn't be surprised to find most jobs are beyond him."

Sorelle could point out that she has a steady job with no degree. She has sometimes thought of pointing out, as well, what she believes is true: The reason Weston cannot keep a job is the same reason he couldn't stay in school. One is not a function of the other. Thinking this, she's reminded of her mother's customers, believers who hope to find good fortunes just by holding out their hands. In place of steady work, Weston spends his time chasing after lucky signs. It's no wonder his life's so unsettled.

Sorelle recalls a story Johanna once told her about a

philosopher who gave a lecture on the solar system. Afterward, he was approached by a tall, elderly woman. "You're wrong," she informed him. "The earth does not revolve around the sun." "Oh," he replied politely. "What is your theory?" "The earth," she explained, "rests on the back of a very large turtle." "Yes?" he said, interested. "And on what does that turtle rest?" "Why, on the back of an even larger turtle," she said. "Really?" said the philosopher. "And on what does *that* turtle rest?" Drawing herself up, the woman looked the philosopher in the eye. "Oh, no, you don't," she told him. "It's turtles all the way down."

Sorelle had laughed when she heard the story, finding it funny, but not sure why. She has occasionally meditated on it in the intervening months. At first, she saw it as pertaining to Weston: "If this, then that" could not be any clearer. He is like the woman who sees the world in motion, but holds onto the turtles. Now Sorelle sees, however, the story could reflect as well on Weston's relatives, especially Leon. They don't forgive, they won't forget, they can't accept who Weston is. They are like both the woman *and* the turtles, closing their eyes and tucking in their heads. Sorelle is not that way.

Sorelle sees Weston as he is, and simply loves him. She understands he cannot live the life they would prescribe for him. He sees himself as free, free to come and go, live as he likes, free not to be bossed, free to tell the man where to get off. Of course, that's why he's free right now, and unemployed, again.

Sorelle, who has never in her life told anyone where to get off, in fact admires this about her husband, though she keeps it to herself. Hard as she works, reliable as she is, she is always being told in some small way she fails the system. In the accounting office where she works, she knows that she's one of the best at her job. She is careful, accurate, learns new routines quickly, only rarely comes in late on account of arrangements for the children. Yet, when promotions are made, she is overlooked. When she asks why, there is always some excuse, but Sorelle, who graduated valedictorian in her high school class, knows how far the distance is between a good excuse and a reasonable reason. Some days she feels herself falling, deeper and deeper, into some dark chasm from which she sees clearly there will be no climbing out. Knowing no way around it, she tries not to think of it. Not thinking of it isn't that hard. Nearly every day presents some new emergency to take up her time, today for instance. Thinking this, she sees a sign: "Telephones, 200 feet ahead." She slows her car, pulls off the road, and stops to make a call.

It is past eleven when Johanna answers the phone for the second time this morning. She looks as if she hasn't moved since we left her, except that now her leg no longer drapes across the table, and in place of the coffee cup a book is propped open in front of her. Looks can be deceiving though. She has, in fact, showered, rearranged her hair, and put on the little bit of make-up that she wears. Except for a rose-patterned silk shift that she will put on in a little while, beneath her long robe she is attired for the day.

She speaks a few words into the receiver softly, then hands it to Leon, pleased that he is back from wherever he was so he can talk with Sorelle. He sits in Johanna's vacated chair, and she goes into the tiny kitchen to put away dishes, raspberry preserves, and leftover pastries. She does not run water in the sink, though, as she intends to listen to Leon's conversation, one-sided though it will be. Through years of her marriage, Johanna has become adept at supplying missing sides, frequently at both ends, since Leon's portion typically consists of single syllable replies, "yes" and "no," sounds of assent or dissent, which must then be sorted out by Johanna. This time, however, he is uncustomarily verbal, and Johanna has hardly any need to exercise her considerable imagination.

"That boy is not going to make a monkey out of me," she hears him say, his tone just this side of angry. She wants to interrupt, say: "Don't be angry at Sorelle." It's an old story. They both have heard it all before. What Leon means is this:

He promised all his children that when they finished college he would buy them cars. Only Weston didn't finish; Leon is not about to buy his car now, even if it is Sorelle's. "He could have picked out any one he wanted." He means the way Eugenia did, and Rebecca. Rebecca picked hers out only last month, routine early rites for spring graduation. Unlike the stripped-down car in question, Rebecca's will come with every extra, including red stripes, hand-painted, on both sides.

Johanna has tried to stay uninvolved. She does not believe in the policy. She believes college itself is the gift, and a car is redundant. She also doesn't believe in cars, although it's true she has one. Leon bought it for her two winters ago, and ever since she has been trying with no success to get him to appropriate it. Last month she read a novel in which a white woman on an Indian reservation in Minnesota was turning into an Ojibwa. The woman walks fifteen miles from her Indian home to her old home to see her newly wealthy son, visiting from Silicon Valley in California. "You should have a car," he tells her. But she turns down his offer to buy her one, pointing out that a car means repairs, insurance, and all of the rest. "Without a car things are simple," she says.

The simplest thing, Johanna sees, would be to give Sorelle *her* car, but she understands that such an arrangement isn't possible. She can easily imagine how Leon would react to that idea.

What she can't imagine, though, is that Leon could concur with Lily's plan. She doesn't mean about the car's repossession, only about the means devised for its delivery. Leon is protectively old-fashioned when it comes to mothers and children. Sometimes his attitude has caused dissension in his household, where Johanna tries to put forth a liberated front, but more often she's been touched and reassured by it. She *loves* to see Leon with a baby. She treasures photographs of him with Rebecca in his lap; slim, broad-shouldered, young, his oversized hands seem to be encircling a doll with Rebecca's bright eyes and impish smile. Naturally Leon is older now, somewhat heavier, his hair just starting to thin, but when she looks at him, Johanna still sees a tall, handsome, tan-complexioned man with wide-set, penetrating eyes. "I have never known another man to take such pleasure in a baby," Johanna has said on various occasions. Nor must the baby be his own. Leon will sit with anybody's baby on his lap for hours. When the child begins to speak, though, it is a different matter. Just at that time when Johanna starts to take real interest, Leon loses his. She has noticed, lately, how critical he's become of Alessandria, and her tendency to blithely skip from topic to topic when she speaks.

"She's only four," Johanna points out, when Alessandria's attempts at conversation irritate her grandfather. "She takes after her father," Leon says. "Always chattering, but never saying anything." Whatever Weston says, unfailingly, sounds to his father like excuses for the son's behavior, behavior Leon finds incomprehensible. "Contrary" is how Johanna would put it, as in that old-time story she used to tell Rebecca:

Once, in a village in Africa, a man took for his wife a contrary woman. When he proposed they build a round stone house, she insisted on a square one of clay; when he asked for coffee, she served him tea; when he wanted meat, she gave him grain. It didn't get better. The day he asked for a basket, she brought him a pot; he suggested they travel over the hill, she wanted to cross the plains. Though at first the husband was disheartened, as time went by he learned to get some of the things he wanted. When he desired tea, for instance, he asked for coffee; when he preferred to travel the plains route, he suggested the hill; and when he had need for a pot, he requested that a basket be brought. So that is the way things went for a long time.

Then one day, during the rainy season, the man and his wife were on their way home from town. A heavy rain overtook them; water poured down in buckets. When they came to the river, it was a rushing torrent. Water whirled and swirled; small uprooted trees and branches were carried in its wake, and the river overflowed its banks.

"It is dangerous," the man said. "We must wait." "It is not *too* dangerous," the woman said. "We will cross." "If you insist," said the husband. "But I will go first and test the current." "I will go first," said the wife, "for I am a woman." And, going first, she missed her footing, and fell into the river, and was lost to view. "Help! Help!" her husband shouted. "My wife is being carried away by the current." The villagers came running. "Where? Where?" "She has disappeared into the river," said the man. "She is *that* contrary, though, it is certain she would only float upstream." They ran upstream to look, but couldn't find her. Time passed, they gave up searching, and returned to their village without her. "You see the way it is," her husband told his friends, "the lengths to which some people will go just to have their own way."

Thinking of this story, Johanna has lost track of Leon's conversation. She sees now he is hanging up the phone. She looks at him expectantly. What is she expecting? If she expects him to reverse Sorelle's journey and send her home, she is bound to be disappointed. "That boy is not going to get me to do what I promised I never would, buy him a car when he hasn't finished school yet." He says it as if there were some possibility that Weston one day would. "Over my dead body will I pay for that boy's car." Johanna refrains, again, from pointing out that the car in question is Sorelle's, not Weston's. Weston has his car. However behind he is in payments, his was not impounded, nor does his grandmother hold a lien on it. Johanna bends over, kisses Leon's ear, and goes inside to finish dressing.

Later, toward evening, Johanna sits at the kitchen table again, reading that same book which was in front of her the last time we looked. In "The Dreamers," a story by Isak Dinesen, she reads a letter from a father to his son. The gist of it is this:

Having recently spent several months examining a collection of family papers, the father has come to the conclusion that the family's success for over two hundred years has been due to the fact that always among them has been "one individual who has carried all the weakness and vice of his generation." Because faults normally divided among many lay upon only his head, the others were spared and could prosper. Now the father has come to believe his own son's persistent disobedience is proof that he is the chosen victim of his generation, and that his example of weakness and vice serves as a useful deterrent to the others. In that spirit, the father offers his blessing.

Johanna pauses in her reading and reflects. Fathers and sons, she thinks; this story has been going on for a very long time.

Finally, we come to Lily, without whom there would be no story, or at least not this one. She is at her desk, poring over her account books, records of real estate she owns and rents. Though she calls this room she's in her office it could, and more accurately, be called her living room. Through the years, she has moved into it a refrigerator and a stove, a folding bed, a television, and had installed a kitchen sink and corner lavatory. Eastward from this room extends the house, huge and sumptuously appointed, planned by Lily with her children and their children in mind. But visits from them are rare and Lily, who cannot abide waste, has taken to renting some of the rooms to female college students. Unaccountably, to her, this irritates Leon and his siblings so that now, even when they do visit, they make arrangements to sleep at the local Holiday Inn. From time to time they have suggested to her that another person in the house would be a good idea. They mean a woman fifty-ish or sixty, though, to keep an eye on Lily, who turned eighty-two last month.

Lily is at her best early in the day. She looks not necessarily young for her age then, so much as wonderful for it. Her skin, light brown, shows few lines and its texture is surprisingly firm, not papery like most old people's skin. She still has dimples when she smiles, and the bones that shape her face are of that mold so prized in models. Her small, even, nearly perfect teeth, the feature she is vainest about, are cause for true wonder when one considers her childhood's time and place, south Arkansas, and the condition of its dentistry. Her hair has gone completely gray and, though she used to hide it under wigs, now its rows of spring-like curls frame her face, softly, naturally. Mornings, her bearing is regal, and that same intelligent, penetrating look that Johanna loves in Leon, gleams from Lily's eyes.

Seen late in the day, however, when her arthritis is at its worst, or perhaps owing partially to the aftereffects of an early stroke, Lily's face reflects the discomfort her body inflicts: Her eyes cloud over, her vision sporadically and unpredictably disrupted by moving cataracts; her midriff protrudes, the result of persistent, chronic problems of digestion; and her posture fails her, pure weariness; then her mouth draws up and tightens, against actual pain, or in resentment at the limitations old age imposes.

Now it is morning, though, Saturday, and Lily is awaiting her great-grandchildren's visit. Her floor-length wine colored robe, velvet, with gold brocading, fastens down the front. It was made for her years ago by a seamstress in Petersburg out of material that Lily carried back with her from one of the innumerable trips she used to take to far-off places. She still occasionally plans such trips but the last several times she has had to cancel her plans, "for reasons of business and health."

Sometimes she thinks her business is a drain on her health. Other times she sees her failing health as a drain on her business. Either way, she decides she should turn over more of the day to day details to some of her children, but she never does. Her children seem so frivolous to her, so lacking in purpose, so *careless*. Even Leon seems careless to his mother. She doesn't understand them, and she understands their children even less — Weston, for instance, her only grandson, who never finished college and who can't hold on, for long, to any job. She sees him as a common con man, charming and unstable.

When he seems his most sincere is when he irritates her most; she sees so little difference, none, between him and some snake oil medicine man in a carnival sideshow. He reminds her of her oldest brother, Samuel, the one she loved the best. He left when she was twelve, flew, like a homing pigeon in reverse, north to Chicago where he disappeared, only to resurface now and then in someone else's bad luck story.

Sorelle is a different matter. Once Lily had seen in her, or thought she did, an elemental goodness, an innocence. Purely practical, Lily somehow let herself romanticize Sorelle; imagined her, rising miraculously out of the noisy, crowded streets of Philadelphia, undamaged by her early life as a fortuneteller's child. Sorelle represented to her a quality that Lily prized, resiliency. In the serenity of Sorelle's presence, Lily took heart. That was why she'd saved her car, retrieved it for her when no one else in the family would, or even cared to hear about it, bought it back, and then extended one year's credit, interest free. ("I told Mother not to get involved with that car from the start," Leon points out.) Now the year is nearly up. She sees she was mistaken, understands Sorelle's no different from her husband, Weston. Lily sees, finally, they are a pair. She sighs and feels her age. At eighty-two, she thinks, she shouldn't have to deal with children's children's problems.

When Lily was the age Sorelle is now, three of her four children were already born, and she was teaching grade school with just her high school diploma. Arkansas didn't require college degrees for teaching in its colored schools; maybe not in any of its schools. Still, Lily eventually got one. She and her husband took turns, going nights and summers, until both of them graduated; then they went back for master's degrees, then more teaching, saving every penny that they could, buying land cheap and building on it. Lily's father had taught her to value land and manage it. She taught her husband. They prospered. She wished her father had lived to see it; how proud of her he would have been.

Her father died when she was in her teens, leaving her a

parcel of land and some money. It was a start. He left the store to her mother: milk, buttermilk, bread, flour, eggs, baking soda, salt, soap powder, canned sardines, soda pop, penny candies, all those things folks thought they needed to get by were sold there. When customers took to shopping in new, larger stores, Lily's mother gradually closed up hers, unlocking it and turning on the lights only when someone wanting something rang her front door bell in the house where they lived, an A-frame wooden building adjoining the store, with a gasoline pump in the yard. Old-time customers still came by, mostly when they needed credit.

Lily is not much given to introspection, but this one thing has caused her sorrow: The week before Lily's mother was taken by a final stroke, she said to Lily, "I forgot to mark down who paid me last week." She meant she had not remembered to put in her book which customers had paid her how much on the amounts that they owed. "I can't believe that you forgot." Lily bristled. "How could you be so careless?" She asked her own mother that. Then Lily watched as her mother's face fell, her mouth twisted in that lopsided, apologetic grin left by an earlier stroke. A week later her mother was dead. "It's the one thing I've never forgiven myself," Lily told Johanna, a long time ago.

Now Lily stands, slowly, and goes out of her office, down the long, thickly carpeted hall to where the building turns north in an "L." Bedrooms open off a second long foyer; each has its own private bath. Lily stops in the first doorway she comes to, and inspects the room with satisfaction. There is a rocking horse in the center, mounted on springs, and a shiny red tricycle in one corner. In a second corner, a new, white scooter is hidden under a piece of canvas, a surprise for Alessandria; Lily has noticed, in the parking lots of her projects, that scooters have come back. Unlike the rooms that Lily's children grew up in, sparely practical, with painted walls, linoleum on the floors, and corduroy spreads that doubled as blankets, this room is papered in a circus design, has lush red broadloom wall to wall, quilted bedspreads and matching striped curtains. Though Lily had the room made over into a nursery the month before Alessandria was born, neither Alessandria nor Victoria has ever actually slept in it. The few times they stayed overnight, both children insisted on getting into bed with Weston and Sorelle, sleeping in another room. Remembering, Lily frowns, then puts fresh linen and lace pillow cases on top of both beds, ready for Sorelle to make them up. (What makes Lily think that anyone is staying?)

Next, she retraces her steps, goes into the kitchen and looks inside the large refrigerator to see if there is something in it the children might like eating. It is nearly empty. The smaller refrigerator, in her office, holds only odds and ends. "Well, I will take them all out for lunch," Lily says to herself, deciding they will like that. (Has she forgotten why they're coming? What can she be thinking of? Is this a story about great-grand-children, or is it still about a car?)

A few minutes later Lily is at her desk, again, her elbows propped on the green, leather-bound blotter, her chin resting in her hands. She looks tired, all her features sag — old age's surest sign, the inevitable downward pull of gravity. She thinks about Alessandria and Victoria, her only link to the future, the final generation she will see. She considers their mother, Sorelle, whom she trusted, mistrusted, whose car she redeemed, now plans to reclaim. She focuses on her anger: at Sorelle for missing her payments, for no explanation, not even a phone call or letter; at herself for being taken in, fooled by a soft voice and graceful manners. Sorelle is Weston's wife; cut from the same cloth, they are two of a kind. Why didn't she see that from the start?

She hears a car pull into the driveway and stop; its motor is turned off. She lifts a corner of the curtain and peers through the window. Sorelle is climbing from the car, helping the children out. Lily goes to greet them. How peaceful they all look. (Are they gathering here together for a family reunion then, or for the repossession of a vehicle?)

146

* * *

Several days later, say Tuesday, Sorelle telephones after work and speaks to Johanna. (Actually, she calls to talk to Leon but, as usual, he is out of town on business.) Sorelle is back home, with the car. Johanna's not surprised. (She had been meaning to call Sorelle since Saturday. "Have you heard anything?" she'd asked Leon several times. He hadn't.) Now, never having truly expected Lily to take back the car, Johanna's interested in hearing what happened, which she does, more or less, Sorelle's version, told in short order. Sorelle, after all, is paying for the call:

"The thing I need to know is what you're planning to do about my car," Lily said over lunch at Morrisson's Café, a cafeteria really. Lily had driven them all to the restaurant in her Mercedes, with its mahogany dashboard, burgundy upholstery and carpets. She had instructed Sorelle to leave the other car, parked and locked, in the driveway, and to give her the keys.

"What really gets under my skin is that I trusted you," Lily went on before Sorelle had a chance to reply. "Well, there's no helping some people. You and that husband for instance." "But I'm not like that. I had a plan," Sorelle explained, or tried to. She was bewildered to hear herself compared with Weston. "How's that?" Lily asked. "You give a good imitation. You surely fooled me." So Sorelle told Lily her plan: A loan to pay back everything she owed her. Sorelle had been to the bank, had it almost in hand; then, on account of Weston's job falling through, the loan did too. (Well, there was also the matter of so many unpaid credit card bills, way past overdue, but Sorelle saw no reason to bring that up now.) "I tried all week to think how to tell you."

"Unh-hunh," said Lily over dessert, large wedges of key lime pie. Then, finished, she drove to her bank with Sorelle. "This is my granddaughter-in-law." She introduced Sorelle to the bank manager, Ms. Gruen. "These two are my great-grandchildren." "I know how proud you are of them," said

Ms. Gruen, shark teeth showing in what she surely hoped was a smile. "Ummm," said Lily. "We're here to get a car loan. The car's in this girl's name. Right now, I'm holding the note."

"There's no problem with that," said Ms. Gruen, speaking for the bank. "There's just one thing—I have to require that you co-sign the loan." "Say what?" Lily asked. "I might as well hold onto the note myself as do that." "Well, that's up to you all," said Ms. Gruen, politely. "Up to me," muttered Lily, standing abruptly and going out the door. "I surely don't need her to tell me that."

Back home, both of them seated in her office, Lily removed from her pocketbook both the car note and Sorelle's car keys. She picked up a pen and wrote on the note, extending it another year, interest free; then she initialed it, and handed the keys to Sorelle. "I'll put a copy of the note in the mail to you on Monday. I believe it's what's called betting against myself. Seems like to me you and your husband play the same game. You say no. I say we'll see. That's all I have to say about this." Then in a different tone: "I figure you and the children might want to stay overnight; your rooms are ready anyway. You can make up your minds."

"Thank you," said Sorelle. (What was this all about, then? she wondered, and still does.) "I guess we'd better be getting back. I couldn't find Weston to tell him we're gone. Anyway, I promised potato salad for the church lunch tomorrow. Besides, I didn't bring extra clothes." (She meant for herself; she'd taken some for the children.)

Johanna has listened intently. She doesn't know what to make of it. "I'll tell Dad when he gets back," she promises Sorelle. Later, to amuse herself, Sorelle will imagine that conversation. Now, she considers calling her mother in Philadelphia, but if she does her mother will only say, "Hold tight, girl," and wander off into some other room in search of her leaves, cards, roots; then come back and tell Sorelle her fortune. Sorelle is not up to hearing such news.

Johanna, in the meantime, is sitting on her sofa with her feet tucked under her and a large, heart-shaped box of dark chocolate creams on her lap, eating and thinking (or perhaps it's called daydreaming). She recalls a story she heard years ago about a girl named Tapingee:

Tapingee's father was dead, and Tapingee lived with Zezette, her selfish stepmother. One day when Zezette was gathering wood in the forest, a stranger gave her a hand carrying it home. Zezette promised the man that in return for the favor he could have Tapingee. "I will send her to the well tomorrow, dressed all in red," she said. "Call her name and she will come to you. Then you can take her." But Tapingee overheard the plan. The next day she, and all her friends, wore red to the well. "Which one of you is Tapingee?" asked the man. "I'm Tapingee," said one little girl. "She's Tapingee," said a second little girl. "We're Tapingee, too," said all the other little girls. So the man went away, back to the woman, and said, "You tricked me." Zezette said, "I will send Tapingee to the well, again, tomorrow, dressed all in black. Call her name and she will come to you. Then you can take her." But, again, Tapingee overheard the plan, and the next day all the little girls wore black to the well, and each one, again, claimed to be Tapingee. Again the man went back to Zezette, very angry this time. "Tomorrow," she promised, "for certain. I will send Tapingee to the well dressed all in yellow. Call her name, and she will come to you. Then you can take her." "If she does not, I will return and take you," said the man. Tapingee overheard the plan. The next day, all the little girls came to the well dressed in yellow. They joined hands, made a circle, and danced up and down, singing: "I'm Tapingee, she's Tapingee, we're Tapingee, too." So then the man knew he would never find the real Tapingee, and he returned to Zezette and took her away, forever. Tapingee went back home to an empty house which she claimed as her own, and there she lived, for a long time after, with all of Zezette's and her father's belongings. She was very happy.

Perhaps, thinks Johanna, such a story can explain the outcome of Sorelle's journey. Not that she thinks for a minute that Lily knows the story. But still, there is that big house, so many unused rooms and extra cars. Lily, as Johanna is aware, is a shrewd and careful planner. She surely knows that she can't live forever. Johanna pictures her, sitting in her office, car keys in her hand, as if she's weighing them (or something else): What will be lost if I give her the car, what will be lost if I keep it?

It takes a bit of searching, but over the next few weeks, in a collection of folk tales, Johanna finds the story of Tapingee. She copies it and mails it to Sorelle, who reads it with interest, then wonders, perhaps understandably, if Johanna sent it because she saw herself in it. (What other stepmother, step-grandmother, stepmother-in-law, is there in this story?) Was it meant as an apology? For what? (Could it be for Johanna's getting time off from her job? owning a car? living in a condominium out of calamity's way?) Sorelle does not believe that Johanna owes her an apology, or owes her anything. Even Johanna's having been born in Rhodesia wasn't her choice. Maybe it has to do with Johanna's being Jewish, Sorelle thinks. (Sorelle has seen most of Woody Allen's movies. Also, of course, she's a reader.)

Weeks later, in a conversation with her mother, Sorelle mentions in passing what she perceives as an interesting similarity among religions: the confession of Catholics, being born again among Baptists, and for Jews—salvation through guilt. (Is there, for instance, some other explanation for Yom Kippur?)

"I don't know about all of that," her mother says. She's busy casting seeds—trying to read, in the pattern of their fall, a future for Sorelle.

Notes on the Stories

How a Basement Impostor Was Finally Disposed of, and a Wife Remained Faithful: (A modern Konjaku tale, the Japanese *Konjaku Monogatari,* a collection of 1,000 tales, being a work of the 11th century)

Though this story is original, its style and subject matter in some ways follow the form and details of the wonderful Japanese, Chinese and Indian tales in the Japanese collection completed in 1075. A splendid source of these tales in English is: *Ages Ago, Thirty-seven Tales from the Konjaku Monogatari Collection,* translated by S. W. Jones (Cambridge, Massachusetts: Harvard University Press, 1959). The story within the story told by Monsieur Jourdan is based on a much longer tale recounted in *The Memoirs of Frederic Mistral* (1830-1914), translated by George Wickes (New York: New Directions Books, 1986).

Bad Hair Day: The impetus for this story, and also some details, come from a brief account in *The New York Times* (January 26, 1988) concerning Zhao Zhangguang, a former self-described "barefoot doctor" who, after 101 tries, finally developed a liniment said to regenerate hair. The Chinese government set up a laboratory and factory for him in Beijing so he could continue to perfect and produce it. For this work he won first place at the 36th Brussels Eureka World Fair in 1987, a gathering of inventors from around the world.

Claudia: Stories one and two about sisters are based on accounts in *Sisters* by Elizabeth Fishel (New York: William Morrow & Co., Inc., 1979). The exchange between the cousins regarding conception is based on an account in *Relatives* by Davida Rosenblum (New York: Dial Press, 1979). Stories about Erin are adapted from an unpublished manuscript by Carolyn Lieberman and used with her permission.

Family History: The story about the fish that drowns is widely known, at least in the United States, and variously told.

The Galloper: The reference to Basia Gittel is from the tale, "The Obsession with Clothes," included in *The Case Against the Wind and Other Stories* by I.L. Peretz, translated and adapted by Esther Hautzig (New York: Macmillan Publishing Company, Inc., 1975). The novel that Louise recalls reading is Walker Percy's *The Second Coming* (New York: Farrar, Straus, Giroux, 1980).

These Things Can Happen: The story of the seal woman whose sealskin was stolen is based on a variously told tale associated with the North Sea countries, especially Scotland and Ireland. The version I find most moving, though, appears in *Icelandic Folktales and Legends* by Jacqueline Simpson (Berkeley: University of California Press, 1972).

He's Sorry, She's Sorry, They're Sorry, Too: The story of the philosopher and the turtles is a frequently told literary anecdote. A version of it appears in *Favorite Folktales Around the World*, edited by Jane Yolen (New York: Pantheon, 1986).

The story of the white woman on an Indian reservation turning into an Ojibwa was borrowed from a novel I read perhaps ten years ago. I wish I could recall its name.

The African story about the contrary wife is widely known and variously told. One version appears in *The Fire on the Mountain and Other European Stories* by Harold Courlander and Wolf Leslau (New York: Holt, 1950). It has parallels in many cultures.

The story "The Dreamers" is in the book *Seven Gothic Tales* by Isak Dinesen (New York: The Modern Library/Random House, 1961).

A complete version of the Tapingee story appears in *The Magic Orange Tree and Other Haitian Folktales* collected by Diane Wolkstein (New York: Alfred A. Knopf, Inc., 1978). I first heard a variant of it, with a different name, from a West African storyteller many years ago.